A Voice in the Darkness

Book II of
The Sundering Chronicles

Also by Mark Iles from Elsewhen Press

The Sundering Chronicles
Book I: Gardens of Earth

A Voice in the Darkness

Book II of
The Sundering Chronicles

Mark Iles

Elsewhen Press

A Voice in the Darkness
First published in Great Britain by Elsewhen Press, 2024
An imprint of Alnpete Limited

Elsewhen Press, PO Box 757, Dartford, Kent DA2 7TQ
www.elsewhen.press

British Library Cataloguing in Publication Data.
A catalogue record for this book is available from the British Library.

ISBN 978-1-915304-57-5 eBook edition
ISBN 978-1-915304-47-6 paperback edition

Designed and formatted by Elsewhen Press

Contents

To my son Robin and grandson Avery

Chapter 1

Sherrif Andrews sat at his desk, staring out of the window that that took up the entire wall, from one lilac-painted side of his office to the other. Two floors up from the ground, it commanded a superb view over the verdant deep-green grass that led from the Sherrif's Office to the forests a kilometre or so away. Deer grazed peacefully on the skirts of the surrounding forest and the brooding darkness within. Constantly alert, they stood just far enough away so that they could flee in case of danger.

On Andrews' desk lay a cherished A4 picture of himself in his naval uniform. It was of the proud moment he had been awarded the Order of Merit from CincSpaceFleet for his services during the Spook War. But while it had been him who'd agreed the peace accord that ended the interstellar conflict, all of the colonial forces who had landed to retake Earth had been lost, utterly outside his control.

"Seethan Bodell," he muttered with a grimace and shake of his head. "We asked you to represent the colonies, and you betrayed us. What happened to our troops, I wonder? Did any survive?"

He'd asked that question before, and Seethan's reply came back unbidden, *If there are, you won't want them back. Trust me. I suspect they'll have been changed for the worse..."*

Naturally the Admiralty had decided that someone had to take responsibility for the disaster and, as he'd been next in chain of command, it had fallen to him – despite achieving a deal with the alien Spooks.

But then what had happened?

"You bastards swore me to secrecy," he growled, "and then forcibly retired me. So much for the honour and integrity of the military."

Until then he'd given his entire working life to the armed forces. Afterwards, not knowing what else to do, he'd drifted from world to world and station to station. There had been a chance meeting in a bar with an old shipmate, who'd mentioned Semillion in passing. He'd said it was a beautiful forest world about the size of Mars. His interest piqued, Andrews had taken a berth on a trading vessel and eventually reached, then settled, on this picturesque but distant colony.

Memories came back with a rush: those first steps onto Semillion, the forests flush with life and filled with bird song, air fragrant with the scent of flowers, loud and soft calls of unknown creatures, and the heady welcoming embrace of nature all around him. If Eden had ever existed it had to be like this. Using the remains of his gratuity and savings, he'd purchased a two-bedroomed log cabin in the wilds just outside a little village, that was in itself far from major towns and business hubs. Now all he had was his service pension, which he'd managed to keep despite being 'early retired'. It would be enough, but barely.

He'd wanted to spend the rest of his days savouring the stunning scenery, taking long walks and breathing in the fresh unfiltered recycled air – perhaps with the black Labrador he'd always wanted and already had a name for, Bella. Trouble was that dogs were rare and the cost of buying and then importing one was prohibitive; only the very rich had them these days. Often, he spent his evenings with a good book, or gazing up at the stars he'd once stepped between, while perhaps having far too many tipples in a feeble attempt to keep the nightmares at bay.

Sometimes he felt like he was falling down a deep hole and was both jittery and hypervigilant. He knew what caused it, the monsters he'd seen via remote cameras on that day so long ago.

Monsters.

Yes, they existed and, yes, they still haunted him. It wasn't just those bizarre impossibly real creatures, but the dead that stalked the corridors of the three ships that even now remained in Earth orbit. Their endless screams coming over the speakers resonated in his ears, as he'd watched unable to help. When he closed his eyes there were also visions, played over and over again, of the landing party torn to pieces by things that shouldn't even exist.

Couldn't exist…

But they did.

The official version of events was that the Spooks had 'been contained', which was far from the truth and Andrews knew it. His infamy meant that, even here on this border world, people soon realised who he was. He should have known that he couldn't hide or blend in, for his name was known and many still blamed him for the deaths of all who'd landed on Earth on that fateful day. To his surprise, however, despite knowing who he was, the locals had accepted him and put him forward for sherrif. He hadn't known about his nomination until, to his astonishment and delight, he learned that he had won the election. Now he finally had something to fill his endless days, and to provide a little help in fending off the constant nightmares and flashbacks.

All wars leave scars. Not just the physical but the mental. The memory of watching friends die when there was nothing at all you could do about it.

He pulled open one of his desk drawers, the metal catch rattling as he let it go, and took out a crystal tumbler along with a bottle of Naked Grouse single-malt whiskey, pouring himself several fingers' worth. He needed it today.

"Fuck you, Seethan Bodell."

Raising his glass, he toasted his fallen comrades, those who were still on patrol. The smoky-tasting amber liquid burned his throat yet he welcomed it. His eyes roamed from the plush wall-to-wall, deep blood-red carpet to the real-wooden doors and furniture, as he pushed images of the dead and the dying from his mind. On other worlds such furniture would be overly expensive, but here on Semillion wood was a cheap natural resource and it made sense to make use of it. Besides, it was an easy investment. He could always sell them later on if things got tough – or he moved world. This planetary product brought in much-needed revenue through exports – along, of course, with the criminal element.

"Fuck it." Andrews leant back in his chair, running his fingers over the highly-polished grain of his desk, while admiring the exquisite craftmanship of the animal carvings down each leg and around the desktop edges. Four-drawer pedestals lay on either side. The top one on his right was the one that held two glasses, plus the whiskey and a bottle of extra-fine Pusser's Overproof rum that was reserved for special occasions. Even now, after all that had happened, old friends in the military still sent him a bottle now and again. At seventy-five-percent proof it was like drinking a hand grenade. It was hard getting such luxuries here. Perhaps he should set up an import-export business for off-world alcohol. He'd make a fortune.

Walking over to the room-length window he unmuted it and leaned out, allowing in the cacophony of birdsong, the lightest brush of wind against his face and the scent of pine and wild flowers that came with it. The herd of deer grazed peacefully on the skirts of the forest and normally such a scene would have soothed him, left him content in his lot. But not today. He shook his head; no, not today. For it had happened again. Lost in thought Andrews emptied his glass, savouring the burn in his throat, and returned to his desk.

The town of Happy Valley held no more than eight-hundred people. Their homes clustered around the village hall, which lay next door to his office and roughly dead-centre of the settlement. Also adjacent was the village hospital, which was kind of handy for when on the rare occasion things got rowdy in the normally peaceful village. Loggers worked hard and, when visiting, were prone to letting off steam after a few beers.

"Sherrif, Deputy Lloyd is on the way up," a voice said from the air.

Without replying Andrews finished his drink, strode back to his desk and returned the used glass to the drawer, closing it quickly. There was a loud rap, the door opened and the stodgy, well-tanned Deputy Lloyd poked his head in.

"You ready, Boss?" he asked. A lithe, stooped man, he spoke in the local accent, as if somehow swallowing his words.

"Yup."

He wasn't but Andrews knew there was no point in saying so, for it was his job to sort this shit out. He hated it when kids went missing, and this was the seventh case this year. A few made it home; some found while others never were. It wasn't the dead bodies but the ones who came back that worried him. There was something different about them. Something that made him shudder.

"Come on Lloyd," he said. "Guess we'd better go see what we can do."

*****

"It shouldn't take long to get there," Lloyd said, as they walked onto the roof of the building and entered a parked drone. Wordlessly, he handed the sherrif a mint while telling the craft's AI the address. Several years back he'd asked Andrews what had really happened in the Spook confrontation on Earth back when, and sure wished Andrews hadn't told him the truth.

He never asked again.

They were silent for a while, apart from an occasional sucking or slurping sound that came from Andrews, as the craft flew silently over long empty roads and dense dark forest. After about ten minutes Lloyd said, "Look at this place, Sir. What a waste. All these damned roads and yet nobody uses them. I don't understand why they're even built anymore."

"Because the farmers use them for driving cattle and moving crops around cheaply. Also, by cyclists, runners, and those of us who enjoy a good walk. Yeah, it's more of a cultural thing, what with anti-grav', but you know the roads are long-lasting and damn easy to maintain.

They're inexpensive, and personally I think they really add to the scenery."

"Still a waste of public money if you ask me. Empty roads give everything a post-apocalyptical look," his deputy replied, stubbornly.

Andrews hid a smile and focused on where they were going. In no time at all the two-seater box-shaped silver craft slowed and gently settled onto the Robinson's lawn.

The two men got out and walked towards a spotless white door. It was opened by a tall blousy woman before they could ring the bell. No doubt, the house AI had identified them through their smart-arms and had already announced their presence. Mrs Robinson was known to have a keen intellect and was on the town council. Despite her apparent anxiety, Andrews found that there was an incredibly warm feeling about her.

"Is there any news?" she asked quickly, wringing her hands while fear – laced with hope – lay evident in those sharp grey eyes. As Andrews shook his head those eyes brimmed with tears but she blinked them back and gestured for the men to come in. Her nine-year-old daughter had gone missing, and she was beside herself with worry.

As they did so a slight chime sounded from the door alert. Andrews noted that the woman's hands were trembling. She suddenly thrust them under her armpits, as if to warm – or still – them. The house itself was of the commonly extruded type, with work surfaces and floors blending seamlessly into cream-coloured walls. The rooms were bloated with modern yet inexpensive ornaments or electronic comfort. Even on this back-water-world one could approve and pay for the design of a house and then, within days, the images would become a reality. All you needed to do was buy the chunk of land you wanted beforehand, roughly plan your building before letting AI complete the design, and everything else was done for you by construction bots.

The entire roof was the usual silver-coloured solar collector supplying limitless energy, while sewage and garbage incinerators were without-doubt included in the house design. If one wanted to move elsewhere, one simply lifted and shifted the entire building and planted it in a new location. Unlike many worlds, where storing rainwater was considered theft, here it was normal to have a water tank built into the garden, as well as atmospheric water generators – or AWG's – which the damp climate helped enormously.

"No news yet, I'm afraid," Andrews said. "As you know, it's all at a very early stage. Deputy Lloyd and I came over as soon as we could. Can you tell us in your own words what happened?"

"Yes, of course," Mrs Robinson replied, her throat working as she fought for control. "I put Mel to bed at the usual time, around eight-thirty. She was asleep, snoring as usual, when I checked her at about ten; but she wasn't there when I went to wake her this morning. The windows and doors were still locked. None of this makes sense, how the hell can she have left without opening any of them?"

A sob escaped her.

"I've checked and rechecked," she continued after a few moments, "and she's definitely not in the house. I've gone outside and looked around the whole area, so have the neighbours. In fact, they're still out there searching. Mel's a very bright and popular girl, everybody likes her. Why would she run off?"

As she talked Andrews and Lloyd's smart-arms, the built-in panels exposed through translucencies in their uniforms, scrawled as they automatically took notes. After a minute or two Andrews asked if they could see the girl's room.

"No sign of a struggle," Andrews said, noting the unmade bed, and that the doors and windows were even now tightly closed.

"Why would there be?" Mrs Robinson said and then, as the penny dropped, she muttered a gasp. "Oh, you think somebody might have taken her? Who, why – where would they take her?"

"We're not saying that's the case, just covering

possibilities that's all," Lloyd replied in a calm and reassuring voice.

"I can tell you now that she would never have gone out at night on her own," Mrs Robinson said. "She's too scared to go far even in the daylight. Most people are. Folk around here believe the woods are haunted, right? I don't care what Planetary Survey says, there are strange things going on out there in the forest. Particularly at night. Think about it, the survey of Halloween detected no life what-so-ever, and yet when the colonists landed it led to the Spook War. Maybe, somehow, something similar is happening here."

Andrews smiled reassuringly. "I don't think so, Ma'am, these are completely different circumstances. Besides, the chances would be astronomical and if that *were* indeed the case we'd have known about it by now. Those colonists had problems almost immediately. I do understand your concerns but let me assure you, this is nothing like what happened on Halloween."

And the monsters that roamed there... The thought struck Andrews like a punch and he closed his eyes quickly to push away the thoughts.

When he opened them, he saw that the woman was visibly shaking.

"The shadows in these woods suck the life right out of you, Sherrif. It's an ominous feeling, like being watched all the time by God knows what. Go on, tell me you don't feel it. Everyone does. Mel's had nightmares for years, but then I guess all the kids do. I can almost hear her voice calling in the darkness. I wish we'd never come to this world."

"So why did you?"

"Because my husband was in the military and was stationed here, at least for a while."

Andrews' nodded, watching her. "Tell me, Mrs Robinson, have you moved anything at all since she went missing? Opened any of the doors, windows, and then closed them again? Did you hear any strange noises last night?"

"No, none of that. And please, call me Ginette."

"But you said that you opened the doors to go out looking for her"

Her face blanched and her eyes widened, her mouth an 'O' of shock. "You're right, I did. I'm sorry but I'm not thinking straight." Her face fell, a strand of blonde hair obscuring an eye. She pushed the hair back behind her ear. "I went out the front and back doors to search several times earlier this morning but that's it. I closed them back up again when I came in and left everything as you see it now. Your man on the phone told me not to touch anything, so I didn't.

"Look, there's her teddy bear over there by her pillow. She wouldn't have left that behind; takes it everywhere she goes. That bear's the last thing her father gave her."

"And where is he now?" Andrews asked, dragging his eyes away from the abandoned and well-worn teddy and looking directly at the woman.

"Dead. He was on rotation to Shiloh when the plague hit. Killed him, the same as everyone else."

"Damn. I'm really sorry to hear that, I didn't know." Andrews said, meaning it.

Her eyes brimmed with tears. "The first I heard about the disease was on the news. All it said was that the Attila virus was ripping through the First Shiloh colony and they were working on a cure. I felt so helpless. There was absolutely nothing I could do and the military weren't saying much, like always. I heard that it killed everyone, quickly. Not one person escaped. I pray that he didn't suffer. I...I truly regret we didn't have the chance to speak before he died."

"That must have been difficult, Ma'am, I'm so very sorry for your loss. I served myself and know how difficult such things can be."

Ginette bowed her head and closed her eyes, accepting the sympathy for what it was. After a moment's pause, she led them through the remainder of the house and then she left the two of them alone to talk, while noisily knocking up mint tea in the kitchen.

"All of this matches those other cases." Lloyd said quietly. "But, still none of it makes any sense. She's right, who would have taken her and why? And how, for God's sake?"

Andrews shot him a glance, and his deputy clammed up as Mrs Robinson bustled in laden with glasses and tea in a pitcher on a white tray. She handed them each one of the clear glasses with frosted rims, filled with a green liquid that was topped up with chunks of ice and fragrant sprigs of lemon mint. The scent of it washed over Andrews, making his mouth water. He wished that there was a tot of rum in it but took a sip and licked his lips, the gentle semi-bitter taste soothing his throat. In his eyes, there was nothing more refreshing than iced mint tea in this heat. It was a colony speciality and yet another celebrated export of theirs.

"Now, you say you didn't hear anything at all during the night?" Andrews asked, taking a pull of his drink before putting it aside onto a small side table, as they all sank into the twin three-seater sofas in the front room that gazed out through a large single window toward the drone parked outside.

So that's how she'd known they were there. Ginette had seen their almost silent craft land.

"I've a vague recollection of music but I must have been dreaming."

"What kind of music?" Andrews asked, feeling a lurch in his stomach.

"Strange. Reminded me of the eerie sounds from those flutes the kids make from swamp reeds. You know, the ones they get from down on the river banks. That music makes you feel wistful and dreamy. Sends a chill right down my back even thinking about it." She shuddered visibly. "But, like I said, I must have been dreaming."

"And yet you remember it so well."

"Yeah, I know, right? But then my dreams are usually like that."

"What about security cameras," Lloyd asked. "AI recognition, ground sensors, house connection history, patrol-bots, that sort of thing. Surely you have those. Didn't they pick anything up?"

Ginette shook her head. "That was one of the first things I checked when I realised that she was gone. The house AI has security features of course but there was only static on them. Last night's storm must have knocked everything out. It was a stonker."

Andrews glanced at his deputy but kept silent, knowing that this mirrored the other cases. Often, a child reappeared a few days later, but it was bizarre how the second child had come back. Five days after going missing the boy had simply reappeared in his bedroom, fast asleep his mother had said. Something had disturbed her during the night and she'd woken. Unable to get back to sleep she'd gone to the kitchen and made herself a cup of tea. On passing her son's open bedroom door on her way back to bed she'd looked in and there he was, sleeping soundly as if nothing had happened. Yet everything had remained locked up, tight.

A while later his mother claimed he wasn't her son at all, he was somehow distant and *flat*. Someone who looked and spoke just like him but there was no go in him. He was an imposter, a clone. She'd gotten so vocal that her husband eventually called in medics and had the poor woman sedated. Naturally Andrews and Lloyd had investigated her allegations but everything said she was wrong. But the mother persisted and then, oddly, the boy's father began to agree with her. Eventually the youngster had been taken into care for his own good, while the parents kept going out together looking for their *real* son. The trouble was, they weren't the only ones. Other parents of children who'd gone missing said the same.

Everything about this is weird, Andrews thought and shook himself, repressing a shudder. There was also something quite off about those children. They looked wan, sickly, and rarely – if ever – spoke. Unlike their previous selves. They became loners. Their eyes turning unnaturally dark as they silently watched you, like endless bottomless pits. Occasionally, Andrews caught a flicker of keen intelligence in them. Of something almost inhuman, something that made his mouth go dry.

Oddly their growth had slowed, and doctors ran extensive checks to determine why. Eventually concluding that it was down to the stress of their experiences. However, none remembered a thing about what had happened to them, or even how they'd arrived back in their rooms. Those details were locked deep in their subconscious, beyond where even the best therapists could reach.

"Ginette mentioned music – remember the flute that boy started playing?" Lloyd said quietly to Andrews. "His mum said he'd never used one before, but when he returned he started playing these really haunting melodies as if he'd done it all his life. He'd sit cross-legged in his dark room in the wee hours. Bloody weird, if you ask me."

The sherrif nodded grimly. "Aye, something very bloody strange about that one, no messing. I don't care what anyone says."

And just when things were starting to settle down, this happens. Andrews had found that discovering a few of the missing *dead* was somehow more comforting, for there was a form of closure. He had no doubt that there was a killer out here. Somewhere. But those children who came back…well, they disturbed him.

Ginette took them around the house, showing them that the windows and doors could be locked, and how no-one could enter or leave without a chime alerting her. She showed them the house security system. It was good, better than most. There were the expected cameras. Heat, pressure and motion sensors that had linked alarms. None of which helped, as nothing out of the ordinary had registered.

"Will you excuse us for a while, Ginette, while we take a quick look around the perimeter?" Andrews asked during their tour.

"Of course, whatever it takes. I'll leave the back door open for you."

The two officers left the house and took a stroll across the ankle-length deep-green lawn that rolled from the back of the house down to the darkly-threatening woods that surrounded the entire street – apart from the road at the front door. In the garden a yellow-painted hover-bot weeded and trimmed the lawn with its onboard tools, thin trails of acrid smoke arising from the machine as the cuttings were vaporised.

Slowly and carefully the two men moved towards the edge of the forest, where those intimidating shadows lurked. Andrews repressed a shiver. He didn't want to do this; he hadn't gotten over his wartime memories and doubted he ever would.

Those shadows, they screamed at him. Whispered in his ears.

"These cases are bloody bizarre if you ask me," Lloyd said, sounding as if someone was throttling him.

Andrews shook himself and nodded. The man had put it in one and there wasn't anything else to say. As they walked the perimeter the pair kept checking the GPS on their smart arms, to ensure they didn't get lost. Skirting around rough, sandy-feeling grey rocky outcrops that overshadowed the town, they stuck to paths where they could, knowing it was likely the girl would have done the same. Overhead, black bird-sized drones whizzed back and forth almost silently, searching for any sign of body heat, movement, or evidence of passage from the missing girl.

After a couple of hours, the pair reached a well-worn track and Andrews paused, frowning slightly. He knelt down and said, "Hey, Lloyd, check this out. Looks like some kind of narrow-wheeled vehicles have been along here recently." He stood and scanned the deep tracks with his smart-arm and then took a second take. "Says here 'horse pulled carts', with a variety of possibilities. I know it's a pain but we'd better follow it up. You never know, it could lead to something. Besides, what other leads have we got?"

Lloyd used his smarts to call the office and tell them

what they'd found. Then he'd informed Mel's mother that they were exploring the woods and would perhaps be back later in the day. They also told her that the planetary Police and their forensics would no-doubt be with her soon and they took precedence over the sherrif's office. She said that they were already there with her. Andrews switched frequency to the attending officers and updated them on what they'd found so far, which was basically the square root of fuck all, but advising they'd keep them in the loop.

Finishing his call, Andrews and Lloyd followed the dirt path and the deep narrow wheel tracks that enticed them along. It was hot. A muggy kind of day in which time passed slowly. Before long both men were running with sweat, their smart-clothing soaked despite trying desperately to dispel it and cool them down. That's what you got for local law-enforcement buying at the best price. The fact that the lowest bidder won was never reassuring. Before long they were soon swiping at ravenous swarms of minute midges.

"I love this planet," Andrews said, as he swiped at the insects. "Although I'd quite happily give the forests a miss. But these bugs are a pain. I sometimes wish I wasn't law enforcement, because I'm fairly convinced that a quick squirt of a questionable pesticide would sort these little fuckers out – and that, of course, would be illegal."

Lloyd looked at him but said nothing, his eyes accusing. In his – and most – eyes, all life was sacred.

The forest was filled with diverse wildlife and an unbelievable variety of greenery. There were plants and birds he'd never seen before. Strange calls he'd never heard prior to this, despite being here now for ten years. He made a mental note to get about in the countryside more; he was missing so much.

As the day drew on the sun began to sink beneath the trees, and it suddenly started to get dark.

"I wasn't expecting this mud, that's for sure." Lloyd said. "Just as well we have the uniform. I always saw them as fuck-me-boots until now. Thought our purchaser was some kind of a deviant, but now I'd shake his hand."

"You know, there's something seriously wrong with you, Deputy," Andrews said, hiding a smile.

"Better call those drones in," Lloyd advised, "We must be getting close by, and I know that any security measures those wagons have could easily detect them. Better something than nothing, though. Still no chance of a satellite image?"

"Lloyd, you know better than that. We've not been able to get one for years, there's always some kind of magnetic disturbance in this area."

The two men stopped and sat down with groans of relief, as a hot meal and fresh coffee was delivered to them by a black medium-sized drone. After they'd eaten they took a break and, exhausted, grabbed an hour or so's rest. The time passed quickly and soon they were ready to move on. Before they could do so a planetary police vehicle arrived and lowered into a clearing, to drop off two constables as reinforcements. The bobbies didn't seem pleased to be working with their sherrif's department and both men carried modern assault rifles. They were looking for a kid, for Christ's sake.

"Listen, this is my area and my case," Andrews told them in a no-nonsense voice. "You follow my instructions, or you can get back on that drone and bugger off. I don't give a damn what your seniors say."

"Well, actually they've already said that we have to follow your lead," one of the two said, with a half-smile and hands raised in a gesture of surrender.

Embarrassed Andrews turned and, without a word, led the party on. An hour or so later they saw a shimmer of lighting and crouched down as they arrived at the outskirts of a camp. Following his orders, the two police officers spread out, one to either side, with Lloyd backing Andrews up as he openly approached the camp, hands wide open and above his head.

Lanterns were slung from both trees and the gaudily painted antique-looking wagons circling the wood fire.

Andrews sniffed and looked again, ignoring the scent of dope. *My God*, he thought, *are those actually oil lamps?*

"Freeze!" a voice called from the darkness and Andrews felt Lloyd stiffen besides him. "We're armed, ready, and don't give a fuck. Who the hell are you and why are you creeping up on us?" Several men rose from the bushes, aiming both antique and more modern rifles at Andrews and Lloyd.

"Sherrif's department," Andrews said calmly, with his hands still up. "We just want to talk to you."

"Well now, you don't need to sneak around to do that, do you." the voice stated harshly.

He had a point.

"All you need to do is ask. Wearing that uniform doesn't mean a thing. Can you prove who you say you are?"

"Naturally. But first, we weren't sneaking up on you," Andrews replied calmly. Then he nodded to a space behind them. "Although those guys were." The constables had approached from the rear of their ambushers and they loudly cocked their weapons.

The strangers froze.

"Now then," Andrews said. "Let's be reasonable about this. You know that if we'd had hostile intentions you'd be dead by now. And, like I said, all we want is to talk. Put your guns down boys, you really don't want to point them at the law."

Seeing that they were out manoeuvred the men lowered their weapons and approached, eyeing the uniforms. Andrews and Lloyd passed over their I.D., which the men scanned with their smarts.

"Sorry Sherrif, we weren't to know who you were," the smallest of the men, looking remarkably like a bulldog, said as he held out his hand. "We have to be careful. There's a lot of prejudice towards our people, and these woods aren't safe."

They all shook hands and, after the constables lowered their weapons, Andrews and his men followed the strangers into the camp; everyone's weapons deliberately pointed at the ground and safeties on.

"You're travellers," Lloyd said at length.

"And there you have it," one of the two snapped. "You label us so easily. You don't trust us and we don't trust you. It's always been the same. So, now what?"

Andrews could have kicked Lloyd. "My deputy means no offence," he said. Turning to Lloyd he snarled, "Don't you know that's racist? More so, since these people reclaimed their heritage."

"Actually, we're Romany," a dark-haired woman's voice said, as she approached from the gloom around the campfire. "Come, join us. It's so rare to have guests these days, and it's always good to see another face. Let's put aside these disagreements and share a fire."

A man they hadn't seen slipped from the shadows and, he too, lowered his weapon. Andrews mentally kicked himself, before following the woman and sitting beside her at the wood fire, her hands wafting at the aromatic smoke. That, Andrews thought, could have been most unfortunate. The man could have easily killed them at any time. He needed to sharpen up. A few years back and he'd have never have made that mistake; he must be slipping.

Andrews noted the tethered horses grazing beside the garish, multi-coloured caravans that were drawn up around the fire. Some of the vehicles looked new and were outfitted with anti-gravs, but most were of the traditional antique bender-tent design that bore wooden wheels with what looked like rubberised rims. The warm colours of the wheels and axles seemed to glow and reflect the flickering firelight.

A long, thin pole hung from each side of the front of the vehicles leading down into the uncropped grass. Andrews could tell that was where the horses would be harnessed while journeying. At the rear of these poles, narrow S-shaped wooden stairs snaked up towards the split-level doorways that led into the dark cavernous insides. The raven-haired woman was clad in a deep-red dress; her dark, painted eyes obscured in the dim smoky light.

"Welcome," she said in a gravelly voice, one eyebrow raised as if in question.

Behind the woman, in the darkness of the forest, he could just make out a curtain of mist. To Andrews, it looked like one of the gateways back on Earth that Colonial Representative Jeffries had described. The man had been quite excited, hoping it could introduce a new method of transportation for humanity, which would have been a bonus to a re-conquest of Earth. But it couldn't be a gateway, not here. They'd only been known to exist on the homeworld; it had to be the darkness playing tricks. He switched his attention back to the old woman and more pressing business. For some reason he thought she already knew why they were there, but he carried on anyway. "We're looking for a young girl, about nine-years-old. Blonde hair, about yea tall," he gestured with one hand. "Have you seen her? Name's Melanie – or Mel for short."

"No, I'm sorry, we haven't."

The way she said it made him look at her again. There was something mysterious about her. What was it? She stood suddenly and gestured for him to follow her: as he did so, she indicated for the others to stay where they were. She led the way to a red-and-dark-green caravan with strange black cursives painted on its sides, like characters from a foreign language. The vehicle was similar to the others, high-backed with a lowered front axle that held smaller wheels – while others held wheels of similar size. Dainty white-lace curtains decorated the small shuttered windows at the sides, giving them another-worldly look.

The woman was about his own height, her dress the colour of fresh blood. He caught a sudden waft of incense. Citronella, if he was right. No doubt to keep the bugs at bay. But there was something more. A heady, additional scent. One he couldn't put his finger on.

He'd been surprised to see the traditional Romany caravans, or *vardos* if he recalled correctly from his military days. They could be found throughout mankind's worlds but until now he hadn't known of any that were on Semillion. The woman's full swaying hips led Andrews and Lloyd up the caravan's few steps, and then she pushed open twin half-doors and led the way inside. Andrews was surprised at the interior, as it was richly embellished by gold decor. Although small, it was oddly comforting. A patchwork quilt-covered bed stretched from one side to the other at the back of the vehicle, and a silver-coloured wood-fuelled stove from which a chimney rose to the ceiling. A deep-red glow peeped from a viewing port, which looked to bleed heat, lay to his left. There were countless mixed stowages on either side and also below the bed. As she sat, the woman motioned Andrews to another chair, Lloyd to a stool. Watching them as she began sucking at a long thin-stemmed clay pipe with a small bowl at the end, from which clouds of fragrant smoke drifted.

Andrews coughed and waved a hand, pointedly.

She ignored him.

"I'm surprised to find you out here in this wilderness," the woman began. "Most people don't come out this far into the woods, apart from the loggers. They say this place is haunted."

"Are they? If many say so, perhaps that's the case. If such things exist."

She looked at him, the whites of her eyes stood out amidst the black eyeliner and black irises. Those eyes, were they full of... menace, or warning? Something. But she ignored his question and said, "I've been waiting for you."

"For me?" He snorted. "How could you even know we were coming? It's pure chance that we're here. We just followed your tracks: kind of hard to miss them really."

"The cards told me that you'd come, and they never lie. They also said that you'd be seeking them."

"Cards...them? What do you mean?"

"I use the Tzigane Tarot, the traditional cards of our people."

Andrews hid a smile; he was used to bullshit. But her next words chilled him.

"You've seen *them* before, somewhere else."

His eyes narrowed. "Who do you mean, *them*? And are they responsible for Melanie's disappearance?"

"The Fey," her voice was a mere whisper but those words curled around his ears.

"Who the fuck are the Fey?"

"Not who, what. But you know, don't you, Sherrif Andrews. You saw something similar to them once, far from here. And you know what they can do."

"I've no idea what you're talking about. What do these Fey want?" Andrews stuttered, suddenly having an idea what she meant. "They can't possibly be here. There's no way. It's not like they have star ships or anything."

"Not every race needs star ships. There are legends from the old days of the Fey using changelings to replace humans, but what if these aren't simply tales to scare children in the night?"

The old woman picked up a set of cards, shuffled them and set them out on a small table before Andrews. "Touch one."

Andrews reached forward, begrudgingly, and complied. The hand-painted masterpieces were rough against his hesitant finger.

Lloyd looked closely; never having seen any cards like these before.

Pulling back the cards she shuffled them and lay several faces up, one-by-one in front of Andrews.

"It says here that you must go on a long and dangerous journey to see something you're afraid of, that which haunts you, in the hope they can help." She said in a sandpaper voice.

"I hope not. All I'm after is the missing girl," Andrews replied, looking away.

"That's what you seek now. What torments you is something quite different but the two – that and the missing – are all interlinked. I know these plague your dreams, it makes you wake screaming in the night. And it should."

Lloyd watched him wordlessly as Andrews tensed.

It was as if a great weight had settled onto the sherrif's chest. He struggled to speak but finally blurted, "You're talking about the Spooks."

"Yes. Like I said, it's all connected. You must go and talk to them."

It was if a pail of icy water had been poured over him. "They won't talk to me. They've told us never to return."

Just then Andrews' smart arm lit up, making him jump. It was the office, a male voice saying, "Hey sherrif, Mrs Robinson's just contacted us to say that her daughter's returned. But there's a problem."

"And what might that be?" Andrews rasped.

"She says that the girl looks like Mel and talks like her, but it isn't her. She's doing her crust and keeps saying she wants her real daughter back."

"Okay, we'll be back as soon as we can." He cut the call.

"What makes you think she's so wrong, sherrif?" The Romany woman said. "Mothers know their children, and if she's right there's a voice calling in the darkness somewhere, hoping and praying for help. You've no choice, sherrif. I know from the cards that echoes of the past plague you. They'll continue to do so and will ruin your life unless you face them. To do that, and to save these children, you must return to Earth and face your fears."

Chapter 2

Andrews watched from the bridge of the colonial fast cruiser *Aurora*. Second of the Pallada class, she was a huge black rugby-ball vessel, named after an old warship that had been involved in Earth's Russo-Japanese War back in the 1800's. As one of the latest ships of the line she was also one of the biggest and carried a punishing array of weaponry. Despite Admiralty objections Andrews had refused an escort. He was, after all, trying to avert an outbreak of war.

"We're approaching Earth orbit, Sir," Captain Williams said. "Should I launch drones and sound actions stations?"

"No. I'm sure that the Spooks are well aware of us and they could construe that as an aggressive act. We're here for one reason, and that's hard to put over when both sides are readying for a conflict."

"Very well, Sir."

Williams' snapped reply reinforced what Andrews already knew, the man thought that his command was being usurped and felt aggrieved. But the captain also knew any dispute with a commodore, placed in command by the Commander-in-Chief-Space Fleet himself, would not be a good idea and at the least bar further progression through the ranks. CinCSpaceFleet wasn't known to be the forgiving type, and if the Captain screwed this up it would be the end of his career. With a nod from the commodore, Williams called the ship to action stations as previously arranged. A few moments later and the ship was closed up, with everyone ready at their stations, just in case things went south.

"Now listen, all of you," Andrews said over the ships' loud speaker system. "We can't afford to make mistakes. We have enough problems as it is. My orders will be carried out immediately and to the letter, without question. Now, carry on."

A short while later the helmsman said, "We're in orbit Sir. No answer to our hails thus far."

"Thank you. Captain, please clear the bridge of non-essential personnel."

After those left, six of them remained: Andrews, Captain Williams and his first officer, plus three others all fully cross-trained – able to do many other jobs – in case of casualties. These were the cream of the ship's crew.

"Keep repeating on all frequencies. They answered us before, with luck they'll do it again."

The captain leant forward and keyed his intercom. "Gun crews, no readying of weapons or overt moves."

James Shipman, the new gunnery officer, replied in a crisp plummy tone. "Very well, Sir."

Andrews had not met the man before, and yet here he was relying on his professionalism in a dire situation. He was tall, black, steely-eyed and impressively built. He'd come aboard during their last stopover, and the commodore would be surprised if the poor man had even had time to unpack.

"Sir, *Rosalon Redemption* and her two destroyer escorts are in view now." The lieutenant manning sensors said, her voice neutral. "Exactly where they were left at the end of the Spook war."

You mean abandoned after being captured, Andrews thought, before saying, "Hail those ships directly."

Without warning the main screen lit to show a badly decomposing human figure. Due to the state of the body, Andrews was unable to tell if it was male or female. Bones peeked through the rotting flesh and tattered uniform; the eyes long gone leaving nothing but black holes in their wake. Andrews fought down his gorge as panic welled up inside him. Memories came back, of what he'd seen before. His heart began to pound, chest feeling as if someone was sitting on it. *Not now,* he thought, *I won't let this happen now*! He swallowed quickly, and silently counted to ten while clenching his fists until the nails dug into his palms. It wouldn't do for him to show weakness in front of the crew.

The only clue to who it was that they faced was the commander's insignia on the dead person's sleeves. Skin, torn in places, stretched back over the face like parchment and pulled away from the teeth, forcing an unreal contorted smile. The thing spoke, jaw moving slightly as if only going through the motions.

"You were warned never to come back." The voice was reminiscent of a cold wind whistling through a graveyard.

"We had no choice, it's important we speak."

"You never listen," the dead thing sighed, and the screen went blank.

On a second screen a translucent lilac-coloured craft detached from the *Rosalon Redemption* and slowly drifted towards them. The object was flower-like, perhaps that of a lilac rosebud or fuchsia just starting to open. Andrews' eyes were unable to look away. It was so beautiful, and yet so threatening.

"Shouldn't we take evasive action, Commodore?" the captain asked.

"Why, Captain? It's what we came here for. Don't worry, it'll be fine."

"Captain, Sir, we're about to be boar–" the First Officer blurted.

Before the man could finish the alien flower-ship had melded with theirs. From somewhere in the depths of the ship came a long bone-chilling scream, followed quickly by a flurry of others and the drum of pounding panicked feet. A klaxon sounded' it's *drrrr drrrr drrr* deafening.

"For God's sake, kill that alarm!" Andrews snarled to no-one in particular.

"Sir, permission to secure the bridge hatch?" the First Lieutenant asked nervously.

"No, leave it open," Andrews replied calmly, before the captain himself could respond. Trickles of sweat ran down the side of the commodore's face, but he simply rubbed it away.

"But –" the officer demanded in a panicked voice.

"One more word and you'll be relieved!" Andrews snapped.

Even as he spoke, a foul stench filled the bridge. The others in the room gagged as a corpse shuffled through the open hatch and stood there swaying slightly.

Seeing some of his bridge crew reach for their weapons, the commodore shouted, "Stand fast! Holster those weapons, now!" Then he added more calmly, "You can't kill a dead man."

The bridge crew silently did as they were told, although each had terrified expressions and began backing away from their visitor. Each knew that this would fill their nightmares for years to come.

Then the cadaver approached Andrews in a slow ungainly gait and stretched out its hands towards his throat.

God, that smell! Andrews thought, as the stench of rotting flesh created a ball in his stomach that threatened to explode through his throat. He swallowed forcibly but stood his ground. Taking a deep breath through his mouth, he said, "I'm here because of an urgent issue. We need to know why you're attacking our colonies and taking away our children, when we had a deal."

The corpse froze in mid-step, the bony hands dropping to its side. The uniform it wore bore the rank of a petty officer, heavily discoloured by stains of decomposition. There was a name tag above his left breast, but Andrews didn't look at it. He didn't want to know. Slithers of putrid flesh fell like flower petals from its sleeves as the hands lowered, and empty eye sockets drilled into him as it cocked its head.

"I'd like your permission to speak to Seethan Bodell, perhaps he can help with this matter. You have my word that we mean no harm and that we'll leave after completing our mission. But these child abductions have to stop."

The creature was silent for a moment, and then said, "Unlike humans we do not break our promises…and it is not us who are attacking you. Your name is known to us, Commodore Andrews. You have our permission to land a small ship at the scene of the last battle."

The corpse turned towards the hatch, leaving behind the foul stench and a few squirming worms. Just before leaving it paused, and faced Andrews once more. "This ship will leave orbit once you're on your way down to the planet. If it remains here, it will be destroyed."

The captain bridled but before he could say anything Andrews said, "One more thing, my smarts won't work in the null field you have surrounding Earth. Therefore, I'll need to bring another person with me for verification purposes. This has stopped our technology from working before."

"What, don't even your own people trust you on your word?" If a corpse could have smirked, it would have. "Very well, you may bring another."

Somehow those whispered words sounded clearly in the room. That said, it turned back through the hatch and disappeared out into the passageway beyond.

Andrews felt the tension ease, as if his very muscles gave a sigh of relief. He couldn't help but look down at the putrescence remaining, the small crawling things left on the floor amidst pieces of discarded flesh. Someone in the room vomited, adding to the stench. Cleaner bots swept out from their hidey holes and quickly cleaned the mess up.

"If you don't mind, Captain," Andrews said, "I'd like to borrow one of *your* officers to take with me."

"Very well, Sir. How about Commander Shipman? He's new and still inexperienced with the ship. He's also someone I can afford to lose at this moment in time."

Ignoring the pointed comment Andrews said, "Shipman? Very well, he'll do nicely. You heard what the Spook said, once our shuttle departs you are to immediately leave orbit – we can't afford to lose this ship too. With luck, we'll be able to shout if you're needed and when we need picking back up. Tell Commander Shipman to meet me in the hanger in forty-five minutes – and to pack a bag for several days."

The main screen showed the flower ship drifting away from theirs, back towards the *Rosalon Redemption* where it simply blended back into the ship. Andrews shook himself and left the bridge, making his way to his day cabin. He quickly poured himself a large scotch which he drank in one gulp, and then began to fill a shoulder bag with essentials. When he got to the transport, he found Shipman already there waiting for him.

Chapter 3

Leaving the ship on a transport was a regular thing by now, as these days most war vessels rarely landed. They were simply too big. The two men had placed their bags in the spaces behind them and settled into the deep, heavily-padded seats. In no time at all the craft had departed from the hanger and was on its way down to the planet.

"Commander Shipman," Andrews began. "I've read your files. You were on the last ship to leave Shiloh, just as the Atilla plague was beginning to hit. You were damned lucky to get out, but those records also say that you assaulted the airlock guards before being forcibly restrained."

"It was a difference of opinion, Sir. In my view we could have saved so many more, we didn't need to shut the hatches on those men that were right outside. They could have been quarantined. And, if you want to know, I don't regret my actions. Only that I had to use force and injured crewmen while trying to save lives. Even we had to spend four months in quarantine before they'd let us land, what difference would it have made to have taken those other men? Even when we were released they treated us like lepers."

Andrews' face was stony. "There's still no cure for the plague, what do you think they would have done with those men? As it was, you physically injured members of your own crew. That's reprehensible. Having said that, I understand why you did it. Seems to me that the Admiralty did too, the fact that you kept your rank speaks for itself. Even if they did sentence you to nine months solitary detention."

"To be honest Sir, I was surprised they didn't kick me out of the forces. But I guess you know there's no chance of me being promoted from now on, though. They threatened me and my family with hell on Earth if I said anything, and so now I'm just biding my time until my contract expires."

"You could have resigned your commission."

"No. I couldn't. They held me to my contract. Besides, I'm the only one in my family with a career now – if you can call it that. My wages feed and clothe all of them and there aren't that many jobs out there, no matter what anyone says. It'll be interesting to see what happens when the time comes, whether they'll force me to sign on again – and don't say they can't, Sir. We both know that they can, and they will if they want to.

"I read up about you, too. Looks like we both got a shitty deal."

Andrews took an instant liking to the man. "Well, if you get the chance, come to Semillion, I have a job there for you, if you fancy being a cop. It's a beautiful world, you'd like it."

Shipman's head jerked back, he looked at the other stunned. "Seriously, Sir? That's very good of you. Given the opportunity I'll take you up on that."

"You're welcome. In the meantime, we'd better get going."

They chatted quietly as the ship made its way down to the planet, and then Shipman said suddenly, "Hang on, Sir, something's taken control of the ship!"

"It'll be the Spooks. Relax, I expected this."

They watched as the controls moved back and forth of their own accord, as the shuttle slipped towards Earth. Both glanced at their smart arms in time to see them go dull as they passed through the alien null-field surrounding the Earth. Andrews felt a sudden feeling of isolation, as if losing the smarts cut him off from the world he knew and trusted.

Andrews' mind flicked back to the last time the colonial forces had been on Earth. They'd thought they had overcome the alien barrier to technology by using troops who'd been modified and highly trained in specialised mental abilities. The field had indeed shut down, but the Spooks had fooled them. As the human forces eventually resorted to violence to get their own way, the space barrier had snapped back on – making the colonials' weapons and other technology inoperable.

It was the first-time fixed bayonets had been used in battle for centuries. Thankfully that ancient weapon had been kept as a ceremonial item and all troops still carried them into battle. They'd done little good though, the forces that came against them were supernatural, and overwhelming. The aliens' trick had cost humanity their entire landing team, as well as the ship that took them down to the planet.

Shipman glanced at his own arm again, his brow furrowed. "That's weird, how come our smarts don't work but the shuttle's engines are still running?"

"No idea, Commander. That's another conundrum for the scientists to figure out when we get back."

All in all, it was a smooth descent and thirty minutes later they had landed in a place that had once been called England.

*****

The ship kissed the Earth so lightly it was hard to believe they'd landed. Only the slow back and forth motion from the wind on the trees surrounding the clearing they were in, and the grass beneath them rolling like waves, showed that they were actually on Earth itself. Outside it was a summer's evening, sun low in the sky. Various shades of stunning green and brown were visible through the forward screen, and they watched as leaves danced in the wind as if performing for an audience. They drank in the view as they unbuckled their safety belts and left their seats. Andrews pressed a button next to the hatch and it slowly opened upwards, creating a shade under which they stood savouring the aroma of the countryside, and the symphony of birdsong that hit them like a wall. Pausing to take in a deep breath of the scent-laden air, they listened as the wind made soft shushing sounds, as if joining in with the stunning melody.

To one side of the clearing the pastel-blue featureless lozenge shape of a ship the size of a football pitch lay silent and broken. Dark-green grass cushioned their steps as they ventured out into the late afternoon sunshine. Ignoring the wreckage of the landing ship, they looked around them, to where numerous insects buzzed and flittered back and forth. Bees droned lazily and pencil-like dragonflies chased a multitude of colourful butterflies. Some kind of bird zipped down and snatched a fly out of mid-air, and then rapidly disappeared again. Squirrels paused in their constant search for food, to look up at them with suspicion from clumps of greenery.

"It's different to see all this in person," Andrews said. "The last time I was in the area I only viewed it remotely. He shuddered at the memory. "You can see why our ancestors wanted to return. It still feels like…home, but in truth it's far different to what we left behind when we had to abandon this world."

To Andrews it felt like the planet was giving him a hug, enveloping him in a welcoming blanket of love. A smile graced his face as he soaked in the ambience, although he said, "I thought the Spooks might be here to greet us but it appears not. We'd better make camp, as we don't know how long they'll be." Apart from the ship's wreckage there was no sign that a battle had ever taken place here. Even the dark protective suits and helmets of the fallen troops had vanished.

The completely-black craft behind them was both small and compact. There was pop-up seating for passengers when needed, or it could be left as a small area for the transfer of stores. On this occasion the chairs were down and the hold filled with camping equipment, tools, food, and water – there were even a few no-doubt useless hand weapons or two.

Nothing like being optimistic, Andrews mused.

Not knowing how long it would take for someone to come and meet them, Shipman fetched a tarpaulin from within and strung it between the hatch and a couple of tall poles that came with it, securing it with ropes and pegs that stretched the covering tightly above them and shielded them from the sunlight. Then he unfurled the sides of a tent and pegged them firmly into the ground. In the meantime, Andrews looked around for fallen wood to make a campfire. He quickly achieved this by using a surprisingly small magnifying glass that he'd brought with him, and which slid deceptively in and out of a small black tool from his pocket. He had a striker of course but he'd always enjoyed this method so much more, for it gave him a perverse sense of pleasure.

Something about their lander caught Shipman's eye. The ship's skin seemed to blur for a moment. To shiver and shift. He shook his head and looked closer. Somehow the sides of the ship were swirling like water going down a drain.

"Sir, look at this."

"What?"

"There are swarms of what look like ants on the ship's hull. Must be thousands of them."

They stepped back and watched the tiny creatures condense into a large lump on the side of the ship, that in turn, morphed into a pitch-black face that looked straight back at them. Ebony eyes swivelled back and forth between the two of them and then suddenly the face melted away, becoming a river of insects flowing down the side of their craft and into the ankle-deep grass. One moment there and then, just as quickly it – or they – were gone.

"Sir, what the actual fuck? Did you see that?"

"Yes. Nothing surprises me about this place, Shipman. There's some really weird shit happening here these days. I guess it's just the Spooks checking up on us."

The sun was setting and gradually the night enveloped them. Andrews' recognised the hoot of owls from the many worlds he'd visited over the years, but then a long, drawn-out howl interrupted them. Cries from various nights bird fell silent, and even the occasional rustle from the grasses and bushes stilled. That call came again, rising from a low groan to a higher *Awooo* before suddenly fading away. The forest lay hushed and even the stars above them seemed to hold their breath.

"What the hell was that?" Shipman asked, turning so that his back was to the craft, one hand moving to hover over his knife.

"A wolf."

"Seriously? That's like a big black dog with a bad attitude, right?"

"Not necessarily black but something like that."

Backs against the open hatch the pair scanned the clearing around them, lit as it was by the full moon now glaring down at them like a giant eye. For a long while nothing moved, and then a ghostly white shape swooped low over the grassland, shot overhead, and then vanished back into the trees. Shipman jumped, as if something had grabbed him from behind.

"It's only a barn owl," Andrews said with a snort, before the other could speak. "They're as rare as rocking horse shit in most places. You're lucky to have seen one. That said, we do get quite a few of them back on Semillion, due to conservation efforts and a rodent problem. They're truly magnificent creatures. They help keep the pests down and are seen as a symbol of good luck."

"Good luck? Unless you happen to be a mouse or a rat," Shipman mused.

It was getting late now and the night air was much cooler than it had been earlier. Shipman took first watch as the Commodore retired to his pit – the military slang for a bed. It wasn't long before his snores buzzed gently through the night air and Shipman finally found himself gradually relaxing.

Just before it was time to shake the commodore for his shift something in the treeline moved. Shipman squinted. There it was again. From what he could see there was only one of whatever it was, but you never knew.

Andrews woke immediately that he shook him.

"What's up, what is it?"

"Two things, Sir. Firstly, it's your watch and, secondly, there's something out there moving about."

"What makes you think that?"
"My gut's telling me so, and it's rarely wrong."
"In that case, we better arm up."
To Shipman's surprise the commodore handed him a spear.
"What am I supposed to do with this, Sir; kebab it?"
"Shipman, if something is out there the chances are that it's more than a little unfriendly. If you want to shove that stick up its arse then that's completely up to you."

Chapter 4

Seethan awoke, his log cabin dark and silent. While his strategies helped with his PTSD, it didn't stop the constant nightmares. It was extremely unusual for him to get a full night's sleep, sometimes up several times a night from horrific dreams – often screaming his head off. He could understand why PTSD destroyed relationships; it took a very strong partner to live with someone who had that. He slowed his breathing and gradually the pounding in his chest abated. Then it hit him and he sat bolt upright. There was a total absence of sound, why? His senses had picked up on it and sent alarm bells ringing, and his adrenaline surging. Out of the solid blackness came a slight creak. Then again.

It came from the rocking chair he'd made, basing it on one that his old landlady Mrs M used to have. She'd basically adopted him when his parents had been killed, and many years after joining up he'd come back from deployment to find that her partner – Alan Wrong, real name Wong, the demented serial killer who'd eventually killed her – had somehow damaged the chair beyond repair, then had thrown it out. She'd pushed the subject away when he'd questioned her about it, but he'd soon figured out what had happened. He'd intended on getting her a replacement years ago, but then all hell had let loose and life got in the way.

Realising that his thoughts were wandering Seethan refocused. There was a dry, fetid smell to the room, one that he recognised. Hairs all over his body rose and a shudder ran through him. He held his breath, listening carefully. Nothing.

Creak.

He quickly reached over to beside his bed, unfastened and then pulled at the string that secured the blinds of the windows. This caused them to raise, revealing glass that displayed the dark surrounding glade and the half-full moon rising over the trees. Moonlight flooded in and illuminated the room, including a shadowy figure in the rocking chair, that was moving gently back and forth.

Creak.

He jumped, unable to control himself. Breathing out slowly, he said, "Mrs M? Is it really you, or are you one of the Spooks?"

"That's for you to decide, Seethan," she rasped in a low dry voice.

She swung her head towards him, those curls of white hair bringing back so many memories. "They are coming, Seethan. They're coming back, so you'd better prepare."

"Who's coming back? What do you mean?"

"The colonials." The words were spoken like a hiss. "Where's that silver freak of yours? Left you, has she?"

"She's dead," Seethan said coldly, knowing that she meant Rose – his android lover. "Like you are, or should be."

"I only came here to warn you."

"And to have another dig about Rose, you never liked her. Your message has been received, thanks. You can go now."

Seethan awoke with a start, his heart hammering. Had he been dreaming? Or could it be that Mrs M, the woman who'd brought him up, had actually been here. No, it couldn't be. The dead were a fickle lot, and they only returned when the need was dire, although they spoke to him when they did.

Creak.

Seethan jumped. The blinds were still up. Moonlight shone like a beam of light illuminating a theatre, as they revealed one of the stars of their show. Only this time it illuminated the chair, still gently rocking back and forth.

Creak.

*****

Seethan hadn't been at all surprised to see the shuttle as it streaked through the sky in the early afternoon. Oddly, it appeared to be under its own power, which meant that the Spooks had known about it and had allowed the ship through the null field that surrounded the planet, and then even to land. He also knew that, somehow, this greatly affected him.

Mankind's colonial forces just couldn't stay away from Earth, it seemed. Despite severe warnings and the threat of war. They were always trying to reclaim this world from the Spooks, who'd conquered the planet after humanity had destroyed their homeworld. When Seethan looked back now, it was nothing short of poetic justice. He himself had fought alongside Earth's survivors against the colonial army that had landed here. He'd fought to keep Earth free from imperialism, to keep it free for those who'd inherited it and inhabited it now. Did that make him a traitor?

He knew the Earth was a far healthier place now than it had been in his own time, before The Sundering, and the pandemonium caused when the aliens had invaded.

When the aliens had first landed, they'd gone mad in their lust for revenge. They'd hunted humanity to the very brink of extinction and destroyed all of its achievements. The day the invasion began, in an attempt to go back in time and stop the war from ever happening, he and Rose had been thrown into the far future when their ship's T-Drive shattered reality. Over those long intervening years, the Spooks had finally calmed down and done much for this world by restoring the wilderness and wildlife. They'd also done what some considered a great evil too, by bringing back creatures of legend. And – even at times – the very dead themselves. But was it truly evil, or was it just another way of ensuring their own survival? Who knew? No one could understand them. For they were, after all, truly alien.

Seethan shook his head. Okay, so the aliens lost their shit now and again. Any race who'd suffered as they had, were bound to. He understood that. But the Spooks didn't just get upset, they tortured and even shredded alive those who crossed them or found other ways to inflict extreme suffering. After all, they could read your mind and then use your very worst fears against you. That in itself led to so many avenues of horror.

It wasn't too far to where the ship would have landed, Seethan knew that. He had to go quickly and didn't want to waste time, for anything could happen to the crew. For the Earth had changed since the great exodus after The Sundering.

He left his log cabin and looked over to its twin a short walk away across the glade. All was quiet. Of the two friends he lived next to, he knew that Eve was out foraging and wouldn't be back until late. Heaven alone knew what Shona was doing, perhaps cleaning the fish he'd seen her catch in the river close by earlier this morning.

He set off across the glade with nothing but the rough clothes he stood up in. Once he was deep in the forest and far enough away from the cabins he fell to his knees, tore off his clothes, and raised both arms above his head – as if in supplication.

He felt it then.

The sudden building of agony within him as his bones began to shift, his skin and muscles tear. Clenching his fists, he accepted the pain; the sheer torture of his body ripping itself apart and restructuring. His scream of suffering turned into a howl as fur sprouted all over his body, his teeth and nails elongating. And with it came the rage.

The feeling increased as the flashbacks hit him. Wave after wave of it, like a tsunami burying him under hundreds of feet of water, as he strove to reach the surface and breath. There was someone sitting on his chest, holding him down. That weight on his chest, the ache in his muscles. He was lost in memories of the past, things that had happened but never gone away. Things that haunted him still. Friends becoming corpses, others blown to pieces or losing limbs. Those screams. He wished it would all stop, but it wouldn't. He knew that. His salvation lay in his strategies, his tools for dealing with the horror. War wasn't like a movie, where someone shot simply uttered a cry and fell over. In reality that projectile or beam punched a hole straight through them. If you were lucky and it was a laser the wound cauterized itself, were it not the bullet left a hole, often much larger on exit than on entry; spraying blood and minced flesh as it continued its flight unimpeded. There were those who lay on the metal floors of ship, waiting for those weapons to hit. Knowing they were inbound and there was nothing that they could do about it. Smiling and joking with the young seventeen-year-olds who so often made up many of the armed forces. Yet hiding their own terror.

He harnessed it. The pain and the memories that accompanied it. The ship he'd flown being hit and crashing, dead friends all around him. Marines he'd served with for so many years. One recollection, in particular, always came back to haunt him.

The cockpit was splattered with blood, both his and Pete's – his co-pilot. The other's side of the craft had taken the brunt of the ground fire that had trashed their controls and taken out their engines, leaving them out of control and forced to crash in the jungle. There wasn't much left of Pete's upper body. Most of it was smeared throughout the cockpit like a foetid casserole.

He couldn't believe how much the blood stank. How he himself had gotten away so lightly – if you could consider the deep lacerations, a broken shoulder and several ribs light. Somehow it just didn't seem right, and the survivor's guilt was to stay with him for many years.

He'd pulled his survival knife from its sheath on his left thigh with his good hand and cut himself free from the seat's straps. His right arm dripped a vermillion stream from the chunk of shrapnel buried within his flesh. The bones grated in his shoulder as he tried to move. Gritting his teeth against the pain, Seethan forced himself to stand, staggering into the mission module that lay a short way behind the cockpit, wiping away blood that trickled into his eyes from a deep head wound. The room reeked like an abattoir – and it looked like one too. The twenty-man commando team remained in their harnesses, and yet so much of them lay scattered around the room, leaving them both torn and lifeless.

All bar one.

Munroe's eyes had flickered to his as she recognised him, and then down to the shard of metal jutting from her stomach. She looked back up at him, her lips trembling as she silently pleaded for him to make the agony go away. There was nothing he could do to save her and they both knew it. Her hands lay by her sides, the chunk of bloodied alloy still plugging the wound and keeping her alive. If he removed it he recognised that she would die in seconds and yet there was so little time remaining. He had to get out of the ship. They both knew it, and those hazel eyes begged him to do the only thing that he could.

Seethan fought down the painful memory of injecting her with all of both their auto-injectors, plus some gathered from other bodies. He couldn't remember how many exactly, only how quickly her eyes glazed over. It must have been dozens.

He became the moment. His PTSD raged.

Harness it. Don't let it win! Use the strategies, what five things can I see?

The grass so green before him. An ant atop one blade, waving at him. A bright-yellow butterfly fluttering a few feet away, only to be snatched in mid-flight by a sparkling blue dragonfly. A leaf spiralled oh so slowly towards the ground.

What four things can I hear? An owl hooting. Creatures scurrying through the grass. As his hearing intensified, something sensed his presence, panicked and noisily smashed its way through foliage in a desperate attempt to escape from what it considered a predator. Close by a stream chortled, as if amused.

What three things can I feel? The ground beneath his paws, silky with damp grass. The pain of transformation subsiding, his heart pounding away like a deranged drummer.

Two things to smell. Ah, the sharp scent of fox urine, the marker of its territory. The meadow's many wild flowers were the perfume painters wished they could create on canvas. There were so many scents to drink in.

One thing to taste. Meat. He wanted that meat garnished with still pulsing blood.

He raised a wounded paw and licked at it, and with *that taste* knew what he was once again. A werewolf. A lycanthrope. A being damned and so terribly feared by other creatures. Yet, also one badly misunderstood. His kind too were victims, who had no choice in their fate. The full moon always brought on the change, although he'd learned to harness and control it through his strategies and, now, he could change at will.

He had to hunt, for he was hungry. Perhaps the tender flesh of a young rabbit; or the rich, juicy, and still quivering meat of an innocent doe.

But never humans, for that wasn't his way. Although many of his kind did so. Perhaps it was in revenge for the wrath they felt, generated by the sudden fear and hatred from their families as they were cast out alone into the wilderness. By the remaining kin that remained alive, of course.

Breathe deeply, Seethan. Scan your body.

His breath slowed on command. The muscles in his hind legs tightened until they were like iron, and only then did he relax them. The thighs came next. Then his back, stomach, and groin. Front paws scrabbled at the dirt, his shoulders bunching and straining. His whole body tensed as he raised his snout to the moon and gave a long-drawn-out howl, knowing others of his kind would hear him. His pack were out there. Somewhere.

There was Angry Andy, a huge black man with a heart of gold. He was the alpha again now. Seethan had taken the position after arrival, having beaten him in a challenge when he first changed; but then he had cast the role aside. He simply hadn't wanted it anymore. Nor did he want, or need, Fae; the Luna she-wolf who'd been his canine lover when he was in wolf form and unable to help his lycanthrope urges. When human he'd hated himself for mating with her, for he truly loved Rose. He'd felt like he was betraying her, and when Fae finally healed from the terrible wounds she'd sustained in that last battle he'd called it a day.

That was the battle against the colonial armies, where the pack had lost Simon and Michael, members whose deaths were felt deeply even now.

When her brother Chris had been badly wounded at the last battle, Eve had begged Andy – now the pack leader – to bite him, so that when the lycanthropy infected him it would save his life. But in making Chris a werewolf Andy had also turned him into an outcast from the rest of humanity, for a hatred of werewolves had been bred into them all from the day they'd been born. It had taken her a long time to get used to it, and to quell her anger at Andy for what he'd done, although she be herself had begged him to do so.

Seethan's graveyard eyes turned towards where his destination lay, and he began to lope towards it; long languid strides that quickly ate up the distance. And then he increased pace, and ran like the breath of a raging storm. The forest was alive to his senses. He could sense the pounding of hooves and paws as creatures fled before him. There was the scent of pine and heady night-scented-stock, jasmine, and mock orange. There was a hint of rain, and so much more. Bats fluttered high above, feeling safe from the horror below, while owls ignored their prey and soared secretly by. Or so they thought.

He loved everything about the night, especially the hunt. The thrill of the chase; the panicked squealing of his prey and the hot pulse of blood in his mouth as he made the kill. The pleasure of the feast that followed.

As he sped through the forest the world fell silent about him, only coming alive once he was at safe distance. It was as if the world breathed a long-held breath of relief. He was death incarnate. A nightmare once seen never forgotten. The sight of him was enough to send witnesses into screaming fits and nightmares for the rest of their lives.

And yet, Seethan wasn't your average werewolf. He was a war veteran. A man who cared. Someone who'd learned to use his PTSD strategies to temper his murderous and manic lycanthrope urges, tools to keep the darkness away.

Sensing it wasn't far to the nearest gateway, he increased speed and soon found himself darting through a watery doorway.

*****

"There's something out there," Shipman said again, nodding towards the darkness. "I saw it move."

"I hope so," Andrews replied. "Bit of a waste of time to come all this way if we can't find anything."

Having listened to them, as he was changing back into human form, Seethan stepped out of the shadows towards the silver-coloured ship. Its hold was open, a tarpaulin stretched from the top of the entrance. There was also small fire cracking away beneath it, the wood-smoke stinging his over-sensitive nostrils.

"What the hell?" Shipman gasped stepping back in surprise, as he caught sight of Seethan.

"Hello, Bodell," Andrews said, glancing at his nakedness. "Long time, no see. You seem to have forgotten something. Your clothes, for instance."

"You know who and what I am, Commodore. If you don't like it then don't look."

"What does he mean, Sir?" Shipman asked looking from one to the other.

"Let's just say he's barking."

"Funny," Seethan said. "How about answering the question. Earth's out of bounds to all Colonials, and you know it, so what the hell are you doing here? You must have a good reason, Commodore. You were shitting yourself the last time we met, so I can't imagine you coming back here unless you had no choice. And, who's this with you?"

"Ah, Bodell, meet Lieutenant Shipman."

"What do I call you?" Seethan asked.

"James," the man replied in a plummy accent, while

pulling a pair of shorts from a backpack before tossing them to Seethan.

Shipman was taller than Seethan, who looked up at him as they too shook hands after Seethan had pulled on the shorts. They weighed each other up. The Lieutenant radiated determination and strength. Good qualities. He also looked like someone not to be messed with.

Seethan nodded to Shipman before turning back to Andrews. "Why are you here?"

Andrews took a deep breath before speaking. "Well, there's a problem back home on Semillion and we asked the Spooks if they could help, particularly as the origins of it appear to be coming from Earth. Let me explain…"

As the commodore did so, Seethan sat down with the others and listened avidly. He accepted a cup of steaming coffee from Shipman, before passing it back and asking if there was any sugar. When Andrews finished speaking Seethan remained quiet, mulling it all over. If the Roma had told the two men to come to Earth then there had to be some substance to what they had said. For in a prior experience with the Romanies, everything they told Seethan had been proven correct. He had a lot to thank them for, and he deeply respected them and their gifts.

"What happens now?" Shipman asked, breaking into Seethan's thoughts.

"We get some sleep," Seethan replied. "It's not a safe place to walk around in while it's dark – or daytime come to that. Particularly if you don't know the area. People have been known to disappear, but don't worry, I'll keep watch. You'll be safe."

"It's not the things out there that worry me," Andrews said with a pointed look at Seethan. "Mind if we lock the door behind us?"

*****

Andrews, it turned out had been joking, and the two colonials slept on self-inflatable beds under the stars whilst Seethan kept watch. He relished the spooky cry of foxes from the depths of the darkness, the hoot of owls, and calls from…other things.

Seethan watched from his chair, as Andrews tossed, turned, and called and cried out in his sleep. His enhanced vision showed the sweat beading the Commodore's brow and the tears streaming down his face. When the man jerked awake it was to find Seethan's compassion-filled eyes staring straight at him.

Another owl hooted in the distance, the eerie cry carrying easily through the night air. Rising, Seethan took the Commodore a cup of water. Carefully handing it to him as the senior sat up to take it, he quietly said, "Bad memories, Commodore?"

"Life catches up with you," Andrews said, sipping at the water and then rubbing at his eyes as if to wipe away sleep. He paused for a while and then looked up again at Seethan. "You suffered from something similar, as I recall."

"Yeah, combat-related PTSD. Comes out of nowhere and creeps up on you like a bitch. It's like being back in the thick of it. Smell, hear, taste and feel all those horrible things that combat brings with it. It gets stuck in your mind, replays themselves. You could get treatment for it even way back in my time, but it's never totally cured and can ambush you when it's least expected.

With Seethan it had been that smell of blood, and the scent of a certain cleanser that he'd used back then. A sound, including a tune that brought back memories of a friend, who'd played it often.

Andrews was quiet for a few moments, and then said, "I was in the reserve Task Unit the last time that the fleet was here. I'm pretty sure you remember that, we spoke after the land battle and drew up the peace agreement. I saw a lot of what went on during that time. The dreadful losses and way in which so many died. I close my eyes but can still see it, watching through those remotes felt as if I was actually there."

"That's called reliving. Like I said, a horrific experience sometimes traps the memories in your head before they can be filed down and stored in your brain, like normal ones do. They end up going around and around until something sets them off again. And those experiences – the memories – are so real, so vivid that you can see, smell, taste and feel everything that was happening around you at that time in the past.

"As for me, I've found talking about it all helps. Doing so again and again helps file those memories down into the brain's library. They never fully go away, but it does reduce somewhat. And admitting you have it isn't a weakness, it's a strength. Forgive me for asking, but how come you didn't get treatment for it?"

"Because of the stigma. As a senior officer, it would forever blot my record, even these days. And what would my peers say?"

"That it takes a real person to seek help, but I do get your point," Then Seethan changed the subject. "You know that the people who remained on Earth didn't start what happened, back then. Your colonial forces did, when they attempted to seize the planet. Thing is, the Spooks aren't stupid – they had you fooled from the first moment."

It had been a trick, Seethan thought. When the colonials finally revealed their treachery, the Spooks simply raised the null field again effectively disabling the colonial's advanced weapons and causing their ship to crash.

"I'm not here to shift the blame back and forth, Seethan, that's pointless. I'm well aware of what happened. As the most senior officer in the area left alive, I was saddled by the Admiralty with the blame – and afterwards retired with an order to keep my mouth shut. The sons of bitches."

"The trouble with the military," Seethan said, "is that we do things automatically. It's the way we've been taught. When they say jump, we jump, and then if it goes horribly wrong we're left to deal with the mess. It's the same with the PTSD, and admitting we have mental health issues makes us look weak, so we don't say anything about that until it's usually too late. Tell me, Commodore, have you yourself actually faced the music and been diagnosed?"

"Hell no. I'd rather cut my own fucking head off."

"Which proves my point, although personally I sympathise. Don't you think treatment would help? After all, if you don't confront those demons then how are you going to deal with them? Ignoring it all until something breaks isn't going to help. Those episodes will keep coming back, like a half-full glass of water that gradually gets topped up with even more crap until it finally spills over. It destroys relationships. Not only with partners and children, but also friends and colleagues. Many turn to drugs or alcohol to get through it, but they only end up getting addicted and that doesn't help."

Unconsciously Andrews reached for his pack, and the bottles of whiskey hidden within it, before withdrawing his hand when he realised what he was doing. They were speaking in whispers, as Seethan settled down on the cot besides the commodore.

"I'll deal with it the way I always have," Andrews replied. "Sooner or later, it goes away by itself. Even if it does take a while."

"But that's the thing, isn't it? It doesn't go away, Sir, it just lurks there below the surface; and I'm sure you know that."

Andrews shrugged. "It is what it is. *Take these pills, you'll be fine...*"

"Can I suggest a few strategies that I use? They might help, but I'm not a professional and I'd suggest that you see one when you get back home. Otherwise, it will end up ruining your life."

"Really?" Andrews snorted. "A bit late for that, I think. But I'll consider it, thanks for your concern." He looked around, ensuring Shipman couldn't hear, and said softly, "Okay, so tell me what strategies do you use?"

Seethan explained about mindfulness, being kind to yourself, breathing exercises, positive imagery to focus his mind on – beautiful photographs he'd used in the past that had helped ease his mind – whereas now it was views he could take in. The use of certain smells to break the cycle, such as lavender, citrus, apple blossom, and so forth. Andrews listened, nodding every now and again, before finally saying, "Yeah, well, I've tried using most of those things already, having read up on them. Hasn't done much for me but I'm pleased to know that it has for you. I'll bear in mind your suggestions, Seethan, and maybe give them another whirl. You never know."

"Aye, Sir. And remember what I said, that talking about it helps too. Trust me."

Andrews nodded his appreciation.

Seethan had noticed that Shipman was now watching them silently from his bedroll, but knew he hadn't been able to hear what had been said. Shipman rose and joined Seethan as he stood and approached the fire, where he warmed his hands.

"Is the old man all right?" Shipman asked. "I worry about him."

"He's fine, just a little stressed."

"Aren't well all? But, if you don't mind me saying so, I think that the cheese slipped off his cracker a long time ago."

"Yours would too, if you'd seen what he had." Seethan replied, and then unable to stop himself he grinned. "He's a good man but, as I'm sure you know, things can get to us now and again. It's something we have to learn to deal with. You never had any issues like that?"

"Nah I'm totally sane, thank heavens."

"Yeah, well, we can all say that."

*****

Come morning Shipman opened tins of self-heating full-English breakfasts for the three of them and then passed them around. Included in the meal was sausage, bacon, scrambled eggs (of a sort), chopped spicy tomatoes, and beans. But no toast. For some reason, even in his own time, that had never seemed to work.

Seethan dug in, enjoying the food. It was the first such that he'd had for a very long time. He stopped suddenly and considered. Surely this used self-heating technology. How the hell did that work, if the null field cancelled all of electronics? He shrugged; a thought for another time.

He wondered whether the colonial powers had considered using chemical weapons against the aliens, but then he remembered the horrific results of their nuclear strike on Halloween – the Spooks' home planet. While the aliens didn't have nuclear weapons, chemicals were certainly within their range and perhaps the Spooks could come up with something humanity had never faced before. The human forces daren't risk a reciprocal strike. Besides, what kind of chemical weapon could the colonial fleet use that would affect an ethereal being? The risk would be horrendous.

"Are you guys ready?" Seethan queried at last, trying to hide his frustration at the delay as the other two men got themselves sorted out. He'd informed them the previous night that they had to head back to where he'd come from and meet up with both Eve and Shona. He and they were a team, and he wanted his friends in on this.

Finally ready, the commodore came and stood next to Seethan, and said, "I have to admit that I didn't think the Spooks would agree to us coming here. The fact that they did bodes well, and perhaps for a way ahead between our races."

Moments later, backpacks on, Andrews and Shipman had closed up the camp and secured the lander's hatch behind them. Before long the group were traipsing through the shin-high grass and towards the surrounding trees, that soon swallowed them. They followed a rough path of sorts through the grass, past huge oak trees, the branches of which looked more like muscled arms than what they actually were. They ignored the eerie cries that followed behind them, and the roars of distant monsters unknown.

Eventually, Andrews paused, looking into the trees on their left, "What the hell's that?" he asked.

"What?" Seethan asked, with a quizzical look.

"That singing, surely you can hear it? It's incredible!"

"Ah, that'd be wood nymphs, or dryads as some know them. Try to ignore it, if you can't then block your ears with something. You get used to them after a while and kind of immune, and then it's as if they somehow know and no longer try.

"Their song feels hypnotic, doesn't it? It's designed to lure strangers into the depths of the forest to live with them. They don't actually harm anyone and they're incredibly loyal. All they want is someone to be with, and to love. They're attracted to humans and try to entrap us, but many victims have families who want them to return home and they often come looking."

"Look at her!" Andrews said harshly. "She's naked, and… beautiful. It's as if she's part of the tree. Her hands reaching upwards, fingers stretching and spreading, becoming other branches. My God, just look at that body!"

One of the branch-like hands had lowered, the fingers curling in beckoning motions. It was as if the haunting music somehow inoculated them against the horror of the reality that they were seeing.

"She wants me, I must go to her –" Andrews said.

"No," Seethan snapped but the commodore had already turned towards the female form.

Andrews had only taken one step when Seethan caught hold of him, signalling to Shipman to restrain the man as he wrapped a bandage from the first-aid kit around Andrews' head, covering both eyes and ears. Unable to hear the call of the music and haunting words, Andrews instantly stopped struggling.

"What-what … what the actual?" the Commodore stammered, his hands reaching up to his muffled ears. "What's going on?"

Seethan tapped on his arm and took his hand, leading him along the path for some time until he felt it safe to remove the bindings, only then did he explain what had happened.

"My God, thanks. I can still see them calling to me in my mind but I feel stronger now, somehow. Shipman, they didn't affect you at all. How come?"

"I could hear them, Sir, but it was as if it wasn't me they wanted. Perhaps they prefer much older people."

"You cheeky twat." Andrews retorted, with a half grin. "My thanks, Bodell. If not for you I'd be in serious trouble right now, I won't forget this."

"Good, I pray you don't. Those Dryads are only one of the mythical races the Spooks bought into existence or – if you prefer – back to life. There are all kind of creatures here now, from Komodo dragons to elves. Be careful, whatever you do. Anyone not knowing these woods is in terrible danger. Just stick close to me at all times. Listen to what I say, and learn."

A while later they paused for lunch. The self-heating cans no longer worked, and so they stored them away and instead tucked into packets of hard rectangular biscuits that felt as if they were designed to test the toughest of teeth. They also had tubes of jam, a paste that felt as if it were supposed to be meat but wasn't, and a creamy cheese that they spread easily with their knives. Seethan much preferred the hard cheese that was favoured by the survivors here on Earth.

"Erm, Seethan," Shipman said quietly. "Who's that?"

Seethan followed the man's eyes towards a shadowy man-like figure in the undergrowth. It didn't move, it just stood there as if made from a light-absorbing black stone. Before he could reply the figure suddenly fell away, as if it were made from dust. One moment it was there, the next not.

"I've no idea," Seethan said. "But perhaps now is a good time to move on."

Come late afternoon they reached a shimmering doorway. Shipman looked at the others questioningly.

"What the fuck?"

"It's a gateway," Andrews said. "I saw one back on Semillion – although I don't understand how it got there. Thought that I was imagining things for a while. I've a feeling these things are all linked, and that's how whatever it is are travelling to our colonies."

"Colonies, as in more than one? I thought the problem was just on Semillion, Sir."

"Afraid not. Prior to departing I was briefed by the Admiralty, unfortunately it's happening on other worlds too. The Roma appear to be guarding them to try and stop anything coming through, as opposed to actually using them. Why they didn't come to us I don't know, despite questioning they've remained silent on the subject. But now you know why this mission was given the go ahead so quickly."

Seethan stared at the commodore, his mind whirling. *Other worlds too.* How many – all of them? But, saying nothing, he simply gestured towards the barrier before walking into and then through it himself and disappearing completely.

Knowing they had little choice, the other two followed him.

Chapter 5

They exited the watery portal as one and Seethan was instantly struck by the difference in their surroundings. Gone was the warm pungent aroma of pine trees and wild flowers. Now he was back to where he called home, and there was a cool damp autumnal feel to everything. He breathed in deeply and smiled, relishing in the familiar and welcoming feeling and scents. He stopped and picked up his clothing from where he'd abandoned it the afternoon before, and dressed quickly. Then he handed the shorts back to Shipman, who held them up in one hand and stared at them, a distasteful look on his face.

"The fact that you could have washed them first comes to mind."

"Until we find somewhere to do so, where did you expect me to keep them? You're the one with the backpack, all I have are these tattered clothes I'm stood in."

Without a word Shipman took off his pack, stowed the garment. His glower at Seethan held an unspoken promise that they'd be returned to him for washing at the first opportunity. But Seethan was right; he had nowhere to store them until they reached water.

Just as earlier, their going was slow due to the colonials' lack of stamina. How the hell were they even in the armed forces, Seethan wondered? If this was their general level of fitness these days then mankind was doomed. Had he been on his own, Seethan would have changed into wolf mode and loped the remaining distance in no time at all. As it was, it was mid-afternoon by the time they reached the clearing that held his home and stepped into the long, cool velvety grass. Ahead of them the clearing stretched for several kilometres, bordered by treeline on all sides, a river running close by the two log cabins. From the nearest building a thin stream of woodsmoke reached for the clear blue sky, the grey smudge gradually dissipating on the constant soft wind. It was still warm for autumn, although cooler and somewhat damper than the summer months. He could smell more rain coming. It would be here tonight, so it'd be best they set off on their journey in the morning – no matter the weather.

The acrid scent of wood-smoke hit them as they approached the cabins, making Seethan's nose twitch. The nearest cabin's door opened and Shona stepped out, walking hurriedly towards them – only to stop and wait patiently a short distance away, as if she had been expecting them.

Shona had joined Seethan's group at the witches' village of Burley, in the New Forest. She'd participated in the battle against the colonial forces, and the psychopathic android Alan Wrong, in which so many had perished. Unfortunately, at the end of the battle she'd expended her magical powers in a mass release by changing her familiar, a crow called Peter, into a Roc. It was uncertain if she'd ever get those powers back again.

Of medium build, blonde-haired, and dainty with it, she also had the most dazzling blue eyes Seethan had ever seen. They instantly caught at your own and entrapped them, holding your gaze until you were released only when she looked away. The homespun clothes she wore were a light-brown deerskin jacket, skirt, and leggings. The jacket was belted in the middle, while the leggings held criss-crossed straps that led down to sturdy although well-worn boots. She had a no-nonsense look about her that dared anyone to defy her. Seethan smiled down at her before giving her a welcoming hug.

"Commodore Andrews, Shipman, meet Shona, a very good friend of mine. Oh and, by the way, don't cross her. She's a witch and can turn you into something rather unseemly."

"Say what?" Shipman said in surprise. "A witch? That's just rude."

"A pleasure to meet you, Shona," Andrews said, ignoring his junior officer and talking over him.

"Not sure that I can say the same about you," Shona replied frostily. With a loud *craw* a large black crow landed on her right shoulder. It ruffled dark feathers, and regarded them with brown pitiless eyes. The black pupils bored straight into the strangers, as if piercing their souls.

"I see you're getting on well with the new crow," Seethan said to the young woman. "Seen anything of the last one?"

"Peter has his own path to follow," she replied, her voice almost a rasp. "Besides, he was probably still digesting the last of those damned invading colonials. He and I are still friends of course, but he's no longer my familiar and nor does he serve me. Finally decided on a name for this one, he's called Red."

"Crows are black, and yet you've called this one *Red*?" Seethan queried, one eyebrow raised. "Did I miss something, somewhere?"

"His eyes go a little funny when he's angry. As do yours, Seethan."

"Looks like a black shite-hawk to me," Shipman added, in reference to the seagulls introduced by mankind to many colonies in an attempt to improve bio-diversity and control pests.

"Seems to be a trait, wonder where he gets that from," Seethan said, ignoring Shipman and somehow finding himself nodding a greeting to the bird. "Do you mind if we go inside and chat?" Crows were smart and he knew that they remembered those who were kind to them, and those who weren't.

As they walked to the nearest cabin, Seethan explained to her who the commodore was. She nodded, obviously remembering him, as Seethan withheld the reason for their visit until they were sitting comfortably in the dwelling. Once inside they sat on wide wooden benches, backs padded with straw-stuffed burlap cushions, a couple of which were also covered with what looked like animal hide of some sort. Shona served drinks of cool clear water, fresh from the well that lay in one corner of the room. In the meantime, Andrews explained about the children disappearing and of the gateway that had appeared back home on Semillion. He also told her about the Romany woman, and that she'd said they'd find their answers here on Earth. Shona frowned, and as she did so her eyes changed to a swirling gold.

Seethan started, staring at her open mouthed before saying, "Shona, are your powers coming back?"

She looked puzzled at first and then her expression brightened. "I didn't realise I'd done that. I was beginning to think that my magic was gone for good. A bit odd that a little comes back with the appearance of our guests here."

"Yup, a bit too coincidental if you ask me," Seethan said, scrunching his face up in a thoughtful expression.

"If my powers *are* returning, that could mean the Spooks see our visitors here as a threat," she said, as her long hair changed colour to jet-black and her shimmering-gold eyes to emerald-green. "But let's face it, the fact the colonials tried to invade Earth last time when they couldn't get their own way would be enough to make anyone suspicious of them. Perhaps the Spooks are using me as a visible warning to our new friends." She raised her right hand to her waist, palm up, focusing hard on it but after a moment she frowned and desisted.

Seethan knew that previously she'd been able to summon eye-searing blue balls of plasma, but for now there was only a faint orb floating above her open palm. Which, in itself, was an improvement.

"I want you to know that we have only the best of intentions," Andrews said in a calm, reassuring voice. "We don't intend any trouble, nor do we have any ulterior intentions."

Shona looked from one of the strangers to the other, her slight smile somehow feral. "Just the fact you are here and still alive speaks for itself, trust me. The Spooks know your inner-most thoughts, as I'm sure you know. But remember, when you've achieved your aim you still have to leave this world. So be careful of who, or what, you upset while you're here."

"Oh, we will," Andrews replied earnestly.

"Note to self…" Shipman muttered.

"As to your question," Shona continued, "I've only ever heard legends of children disappearing like that in the past, but never known about it happening in reality. It's said that the faery folk took them. Tell me, did any of them come back?"

"A few have, but they were different somehow. Weirder, and not really themselves. Bizarrely, the mothers claim the children aren't theirs. Now, would you mind telling us what it is that you *do* know – about these legends?" Andrews asked, one eyebrow raising quizzically as he watched her hair and eyes transform back and forth from one colour to another.

"It sounds to me like it's The Golden Ones you're having problems with, those you may know as the Fey. The children who returned could be changelings, imposters planted by the Fey while the real children remain their prisoner."

"I didn't understand any of what you just said," Shipman said, a puzzled expression on his face.

"What's the matter, didn't you have a childhood?" Shona said to the lieutenant, exasperated. "The Fey are many races of unnatural folk from pre-history, who sought refuge in a world parallel to this one as human kind began to dominate the planet."

Shipman's deep bass voice rumbled. "You mean like…elves, fairies?" He shook his head in denial and then turned to the Commodore, saying. "Well, I can see that this was a wasted journey."

Glancing at him the commodore replied curtly, "An elven army destroyed a lot of our troops not so long ago, Shipman. Let's just listen to what she has to say. It can't hurt."

Shipman huffed slightly, as he eyed Shona's hair. "That's a weird thing you're doing by the way. As far as I know only androids can change their hair and eye colour. Allegedly, you're not one."

"No, I'm not. As Seethan told you, I'm a witch. And

for your information the fey are far more than fairies, and are certainly real. When the Spooks brought them back from mythology after the Sundering, along with many other…things, there was peace for a while. Now, however, they've split and there are two groups of them – the fairy and faery, the latter are much darker.

The door opened and Eve came in, the heads of a brace of ducks poking from a shoulder bag. About the same build as Shona, Eve and her brother Chris had been the first people Seethan had met when he'd arrived in this time period. They'd been with Jon, their cousin, who was killed in the great battle alongside many of their friends.

Eve hugged Seethan and kissed his cheek before being introduced to the others Then she walked over to the sink to pluck the birds, while listening to them all talk.

"Whose mythology?" Shipman persisted.

"Human of course. The Seelie – or fairy – are usually considered kind, while the Unseelie – or faery – are the exact opposite. But, that said, there is a measure of each in both. The Unseelie have been known to abduct children and replace them with changelings, those creatures I mentioned who look human but aren't. Occasionally they returned the original children and claimed back the changelings. No idea why."

Andrews turned to Shipman, a strange look on his face. "Well, I guess that kind of fits in with what we already have." He looked back to Shona, "Anything else?"

She shook her head. "Not at the moment."

Andrews began staring at the wooden flooring, as if mesmerised. He seemed to ground himself by tapping his shoes against the wooden deck; back home on Semillion his own log cabin was thickly carpeted. Now his feet brought the distinct sound and musical overtones of wood-wealth, while his thumbs rubbed the table's surface.

Shona stood and replaced their drinks with a hot beverage that she quickly made with water boiling in a pot over the open fire.

Andrews refocused and sniffed at the steam from his drink, staring into the cup. "Thanks, but…what is it?"

"Mint and cucumber tea; relaxing and very good for you. Helps soothe the stomach as well. Now, tell me why is it the Spooks allowed you to land?"

"Well, as I told you, the Romany lady said we'd find our answers here on Earth. When we arrived in orbit I asked the Spooks if we could visit our homeworld, explained why we needed to. And then we made a deal, you see."

"What kind of deal?"

Andrews looked at her calmly. "I can't break that confidentiality, our very presence here depends on it and I suspect that if we did the Spooks would find out."

"I respect that, Commodore. Very well, then let me tell you what I know of the dissolution of the Fey. How the one group became two."

Soon they were lost in Shona's rough but softly-droning and hypnotic voice.

*****

From the collection of small thatched houses, subdued candle light bled through the windows of various colours, casting a warm beacon of light towards the surrounding paths, grass, and the forest that lay beyond. Out of the darkness, a small glowing human-like shape with transparent butterfly wings veered left and then right, up and down as it flew between the buildings. Finally, it entered a dwelling through a half-open window. Against one wall of the dimly lit room lay a log fire in an open hearth, the flames crackling and spitting like an angry cat. A small, well-worn table and chairs sat alongside bookcases brimming with well-thumbed volumes. Pausing to rest upon the window sill, the fairy Willow surveyed the room. She could hear the babble of laughter from the pub close by, joined occasionally by raucous singing and a badly out of tune harmonica. Her gaze wandered over the rows and rows of leather-clad books, eyes widening with anticipation and wariness.

The breath caught in her throat as she caught sight of a

faint black glimmer that betrayed a secret concealed against prying eyes. Alas, it was not fully hidden from her magic. She fluttered upwards and towards that dark corner, where she paused in mid-flight. Her eyes caught sight of thickly-stranded cobwebs, from which long segmented black hairy legs hung like huge bent pipe cleaners in one corner. She peered closer, her wand brightening and casting just enough light to banish the darkness therein. At the top of the bent front legs she could see the pedipalps, multiple eyes, and jaws from which venom dripped in anticipation.

Willow could have changed back to a normal human's size with a simple wave of her wand but, instead, she reached inside her satchel and withdrew a small white leather bag. From within it she pulled out a handful of dust. Blowing gently at the conker, jasmine, and lavender concoction she coated the lurking creature – in particular the legs, in which its sense of smell was generated. Those legs shook suddenly and withdrew. There was a loud hiss, and then a quick glimpse of the obsidian beast as it scuttled away to find an alternate darker and safer corner. With a few words and another wave of Willow's wand the web fell away, leaving the path clear. She knew how often fairy folk fell to spiders, and she shuddered at the thought of such a horrible fate.

The light from Willow's wand increased as she neared the dark glimmer, revealing – as she'd hoped – a polished piece of jet. Delighted, she snatched it up and stuffed it into her satchel, replacing it with a nub of gold from the same bag. Quickly withdrawing to a safer distance, she looked about again. There was something else here, she could sense it. Her eyes followed the moths, as they danced in erratic aerial displays, wary of the webs that could so easily entangle them. Wondering what was enticing them, Willow made her way carefully through the bumbling beasts.

A hint of cerulean blue buried high upon the top shelf caught her eye. Eyebrows furrowing and wings fluttering in haste, Willow rose until she was parallel to it. A flowerful wave and a light appeared at the end of her wand, revealing a walnut-sized sapphire. The jewel was so perfect it took her breath away. Gasping with delight she reached in and took hold of the stone in both hands, eyes widening at its majestic colour.

This would make a fine tribute to Queen Tiandra, who she knew would love it. Willow exchanged the stone for her last – and largest – piece of gold. Despite the size of the gem it was quickly swallowed within her bottomless bag. Struggling with the sudden weight she fluttered in stops and starts out of the window and back towards the forest beyond.

Into the woods she flew, over secret glades, murky swamps and fallen trees, musky scented mushrooms and sultry aromatic flowers. The hushed forest was dark and threatening throughout. A large brown toad with pale stripes and hooded orange eyes lashed a thick red tongue at her, but she had seen him and easily evaded the clumsy attempt.

It was a long way to the palace, and Willow was tiring quickly, making her wonder if she'd could make it tonight, or would have to rest. A hornet with bright golden bands pursued her for a few moments, until a wave of her wand led it off in a false direction. Those were the worst, the hornets. If you didn't keep your eyes open they'd snatch you right out of the air, and their sting is deadly. Either way, once carried back to their nest there was little chance of survival.

Something moved below her, a rustling coming from crisp dark leaves. She paused in mid-flight and peered closer. Stems of grass were thrust aside as something lumbered through the undergrowth. A stag beetle! The colour of burnished bronze, it had mandibles almost the same length as its body. Luckily, they were friendly, and Willow knew this one personally. With a cry of delight, she dropped to the forest floor and rapped on the creature's armoured head with the knuckles of her right hand, a routine long practiced between the two races. The beetle shook its great head and allowed her to sit comfortably upon its back, and then followed her instructions and crashed through the undergrowth like a small tank.

In no time at all they were there, The City of Everlasting Change gleaming like snow in the moonlight. Its spires stretched towards the tree tops and stars beyond, the single building shone like a beacon of hope in the darkness. The sound of haunting music grew louder as she drew near. Fiddles screeched like demented cats, pipes shrieking in accompaniment. One moment daunting, frightening and a little terrifying, the melody swiftly became uplifting and Willow's heart swelled with love, pride, and joy.

She passed the ever-watchful guards and then immediately into the great hall, where she paused to grin delightedly at the dancers. It was like looking at a multi-glass-floored venue. On each level distinctly-different coloured fairies pirouetted and swayed to the sound, red above yellow, above blue and green; violet then lavender. Others were as white as snow. The levels suddenly swooped together and merged without warning, becoming a cascade of colour that mixed and rolled like the waves of a boiling sea. There was a clash of thunder and a light so bright the entire hall was illuminated for a few moments, before the forked lightning flickered out and with it the music.

In the sudden silence, the dancers dispersed into the crowded audience that bloated the hall floor. Self-consciously Willow fluttered down to the hall and approached the throne from the beginning of the long vermillion carpet. Thousands of eyes, both fey and animal, watched her.

Straight as an arrow, the carpet swept endlessly towards the throne from the far end of the hall; until, at length she stood and bowed before Queen Tiandra. Her majesty's wings were whiter than frost, her skirts a light-green interspaced with downward slashes of brown – both of which bore the sacred symbols of the fey. Her bodice, also white, was thinly bordered by the same green.

The throne upon which she sat was a darkness so intense that one could just make out the narrow oval shape of its back. From that cushioned darkness a profusion of stars caught the eye; a spiral galaxy, bright and blue as sapphire held up to the moonlight. Branches sprang from the side of the throne, displaying a profusion of gold, red, and brown autumn leaves. And yet, oddly, the same branches were also filled with spring and summer blossom, deep-green holly with berries like drops of blood. It was as if there were a clash of both winter and summer. Even raspberries and blackberries, apples, cherries, and pears dangled invitingly.

The queen's intense-blue eyes beamed down at her. "What is it that brings you before me, child?"

"A gift, your Majesty. From one of your loyal fairy folk to her sovereign." Willow reached into her satchel and withdrew the deep-blue sapphire with an air of pride and held it out to the monarch with both hands.

A collective gasp sighed through the hall, echoing and re-echoing like the shush of a gentle breeze. The Queen stood, her mouth gaping open and eyes bright with delight as she reached for the crystal with both hands. But, as Willow leant forward to pass her the gift, her satchel fell open and the piece of jet spilled out onto the floor with a clatter.

"What is the meaning of this!" screeched a voice from behind Willow. It was Mab, the queen's sister, face twisted with rage. "Jet belongs to me, it's *my* stone! How dare you keep it for your own. Are you taunting me?"

"But, no…this is for you, Princess," Willow stuttered. "Out of respect I was offering our queen her gift first. My intent was indeed to give this to you afterwards."

Tiandra tried to say something but Mab flowed across the red-carpeted floor until she stood beside her, her voice a deep and threatening hiss. "Don't interrupt me sister. We may be twins, but the peace between us wrought by our father before he died states we must be equally honoured – even if I was born second. It was dropped accidentally and the fact that that this…this imp of a girl, would take what is mine for her own is beyond condemnation. I demand her life!"

"No!" the queen thundered. "There is no evidence that was her intention. Give her a chance to speak. Go on, child, explain yourself."

Willow's voice quivered, as she said, "As I mentioned, my lady, my purpose was to gift you this wonderful sapphire and then afterwards to present this delightful jet to Princess Mab, as is right. I am well aware how much she covets these gems and I thought these gifts to you both would be appreciated."

"You're lying!" Mab thundered inches away, spittle flecking Willow's face. "Do you honestly think I can be fooled so easily? And look how much my sister's gem far outweighs mine. You insult me, and for that you will die."

"I say nay!" the queen bellowed, stamping her dainty foot. "If you cannot control yourself dear sister, then you deserve no gifts brought with such good intent." With a wave of her wand and a snap the jet disappeared.

A rush of unease swept through the great hall. Huge black rats bearing dark fey knights edged forwards, only to be held back by the queen's red-seashell clad guards who rushed in like an erupting spray of blood to protect her – their long, thin lances giving even the evil ones pause.

"You dare!" Mab thundered at the queen. "Not only am I insulted by the size of this offering, which I've no doubt this wretch intended keeping for herself – but then sister, you yourself steal it from me!" With a wave of her pitch-black wand and a guttural curse, a tide of darkness flashed towards Willow. But before it could wash over her Tiandra raised her own wand and light banished the dark bolt. Willow fell back, shrieking and shivering in fear.

"Please, I didn't mean any offence! This is all a dreadful mistake."

The queen rushed to Willow's side and helped her to her feet. Her touch was soothing; and then Tiandra turned back to her sister, her eyes filled with fury. "I won't have this, Mab. Fey do not attack Fey, you know that! Leave this realm before I forget that you're my sister. Leave, and do not return unless you are invited."

Mab clenched snow-white fists, and her words snapped as if individually furnaced. "You may forbid me from killing her, sister, but I do – as a princess – have the power to banish her from this court, before I leave to create a court of my own." She stamped her feet in fury and there was a sudden rumble as masonry began to fall around them. "I will take those of my folk to a Winter Court, while you rule the Summer. Seelie are you, Unseelie am I; there is now a gulf between us. This thief took gems from the humans, who I suspect are in league with her. That gem should have come to me by right. For her attempted theft, both she and the humans will pay!"

Tiandra stood and held out her hands beseechingly. "Mab, I feel you've been waiting for a reason to form your own court, and this is it. But, please, listen to me. Don't do this. I do not wish any conflict with you, for we are family! But if needs be I *will* stand against you with regard to mankind. You will *not* harm them; they are innocent in this."

"Then there is only one thing left to be said, sister. I withdraw what magic I may from the humans, they will no longer have much of the powers they once enjoyed. Their magicians will fall, become barren and empty of the light. Goodbye, Sister. Until we meet again." Mab turned and strode down the great hall with masonry crumbling and falling behind her.

As Mab left the queen looked down at Willow. "You too must go, for you may no longer remain by my side or in this court. I'm sorry, but even I can't over-ride Princess Mab's decision to banish you. She is, after all, royalty. I must go now to prepare the Seelie for the darkness that is to come."

*****

"And that's how it all started," Shona said quietly. "It was a terrible misunderstanding, which is often the case in such matters. How that could lead to this is beyond me, but I guess that's families for you. Despite attempts to heal the rift the anger continues."

"So, Mab's leading the bad guys and we need to get in touch with the Queen. Perhaps she can help us out in this matter," Andrews said.

"Maybe, but I wouldn't count your chickens. Personally, I can't see how anything you say could lead to an end to this confrontation. I suggest we leave at first light."

Chapter 6

Andrews had stepped out from the log cabin for a moment in the early evening. He sat on a bare wooden stool and took a long pull from the small metal flask hidden within his clothing. The commodore watched as the stars slowly awakened, adding their jewelled glitter to the panorama of the dying crimson and gold skyline. A little while later he returned to the cabin, a frown below crinkled eyes and tightly pressed lips.

"I just saw him again," he said. "Out there on the treeline."

"Who?" asked Seethan, looking up from his seat, as he tested the blade of his matt-black Fairbairn-Sykes knife with his thumb. He loved the long, thin, deadly blade; it was the ideal weapon for close in fighting or silencing sentries.

"That shadowy figure of a man we've been seeing on and off. He was barely visible in the fading light but he was definitely there. He stood watching me for several moments and then, just like before, he disappeared."

Before anyone else could reply, Eve said with her brown eyes on Andrews', "What makes you think it's a he?"

Surprised, Andrews said, "I don't know; just a feeling I guess."

"Who are you guys talking about?" Shona inquired.

"A figure we keep seeing in the distance. Someone's been watching us for days," Andrews said.

"I've seen it too, several times in fact. While we were on our way here. But each time I looked directly at it the figure somehow faded away. One moment he'd be there, the next not. Didn't seem to be much of a threat, though." Seethan said.

"Not a threat? How would you know that?" Eve snapped, one hand clasping a knife the length of her forearm sheathed on the belt at her waist.

Seethan shrugged and half-smiled. "Well, because it wasn't shouting or throwing anything nasty at us, was it. Why start a fight for no reason?"

"And you didn't smell this person with that hypersensitive snout of yours?"

Seethan frowned. "No, there was nothing out of the ordinary; which is odd I'll admit. I can usually smell people well before they arrive, or animals and such like. I've been wondering if it could be one of the Spooks. It's not their normal modus operandi, however – or their way of working, that is."

It was Shona who said. "Yes, it could be the Spooks but, to be honest, I sincerely doubt it. Like Seethan says, it's not like them. What about the pack, where are they now? We could do with them here protecting us, as they have in the past."

"Ah, now that would be nice. I could call to them but, to be honest, I'm not sure they'd hear me. I sense that they are quite a distance away."

"In which case I suggest we get some sleep while we can," Shona replied. "We need to be rested and fully alert tomorrow, we have a long journey ahead of us."

*****

At sunrise they ate a meal of steaming hot oats mixed with crisp diced apple. Before leaving, the group cleaned the dishes and put out the fire. It wouldn't be good for the place to burn down in their absence. Shona led them in single file when they left, heading back the way that Seethan and the others had come from the previous day. There was no sign of the mysterious stranger and eventually they reached the glimmering gateway. Before they could enter, however, a dark shadowy figure stepped slightly out of the shadows and into their path. Instantly they snatched up their spears and long-bladed knives and held them in defensive positions.

Due to this strange ability to appear out of nowhere and likewise disappear, it was without doubt the person that had been watching them. Seethan tried to stare at their visitor in wonder, still unable to fully see him. He swallowed and spoke quickly to the others.

"Put your weapons away, all of you. Shona, how's that plasma trick of yours coming along?"

"Not so much as a spark," she replied tightly, from behind him.

"Then stay back with the others." He took a step forward until he was close enough to touch the strange figure. "Greetings. We've seen you watching us from time to time. Can I ask what it is that you are looking for, and if we can help?"

Until now the dark figure had remained completely still but, suddenly, that chest rose and fell, and the words when they came were unnatural; the breaths sucked in and spouted out like someone learning to play a wind-blown instrument. They still couldn't see him clearly.

"We came to explain that it wasn't our fault."

"What wasn't?" Seethan replied. "Can you step more into the light a bit? That's it, thanks."

"I don't want to scare you."

"You won't," Seethan said, and the figure moved into the sunlight.

"Good grief," Shipman gasped from behind him. "Is that...?"

"Yes. This isn't a man. It's shaped to look like one sure, but he's made up entirely of ants, or something like. Don't forget that this place is now very different to what you Colonials left. We're finding new things all the time."

The colony's chest rose and fell, and again came that eldritch voice. "The Dark Ones' took control of us and forced us to work for them. We'd seen humans before but had no interaction with them, our races just let each other be. We knew what we were being forced to do but couldn't do anything about it, we swear. We want to make amends, if we can and you'll let us. We want revenge."

"Explain yourself," Seethan said.

"We recall being forced to attack a human settlement. It was night and so they didn't see us coming. We rolled like a wave through their village, devouring everything. There were no survivors, only the bones are left. We regret this."

Seethan found himself stepping backwards, but he already knew it would be too late if this thing wished to attack. And even if he could, how would he defend himself against it? There was also the question of the others, they wouldn't stand a chance no matter how fast they ran. As if to drum this home a dark cloud rose from the forest floor and he realised that it was a separate column of – this time – flying ants. They came together like two rivers merging. This didn't make sense to Seethan. As he understood it, ants only swarmed in spring come summer.

"What's to stop you attacking us again?"

"It won't happen again. The Golden Ones worked their own magic against the Dark Ones, and they freed us from their control. We wanted no part of this conflict, for not only didn't it concern us but we weren't even aware of it. We despised the fact that we were used as a weapon without our consent, to be forced into something like this is despicable. Nor do not want war with the humans."

"Okay but how can you form a human shape, and speak, if you're made up completely of ants?" Seethan asked.

The breathy voice came again. "When we…absorbed the villagers, we began to understand how their bodies worked. We emulated one, what you see in front of you is an entire nest."

"By absorbed you mean…?" Shipman asked from behind Seethan.

"We digested them and through that process learned your words. As I've said, for this attack we are truly sorry. We only became aware of what we'd done when we recovered.

"Knowing now your words we created this form to make contact with you and try to apologise, in the hope that you would understand and forgive us. We want you to know that you are safe from us, the Unseelie are blocked and cannot control us again. We want to atone for our crime by helping you in any way that we can, as well as seeking revenge against the Dark Ones."

"Well, thanks for telling us what happened," Seethan said, repressing a shudder and visualising what pain and horror the villagers must have suffered. "Understanding all this helps us but there's nothing to forgive, if what you say is true then you were used. But, what of other villages, are they under attack too?"

"Yes, but the Dark Ones had to use others against those," came the wheezing reply. "As we understand it, one other village was overrun with slugs. They didn't hurt the humans but they devoured every piece of grain and other harvest they had. They covered every surface, including the humans from head to toe. The villagers ran away, screaming as if they'd gone mad. Truth be told, they had to move as nothing remained for them to eat. We know also that rats were used in the attacks, and probably other creatures too, as the battle between good and evil ebbs and flows."

"These Seelie you mentioned – the good guys – are they battling directly with the Unseelie?" Andrews queried.

"We don't know if they physically fight each other," the ant man replied.

"I've not heard of any direct conflict, either," Shona interjected. "I guess they're only working through third parties. Hopefully the good guys are winning."

"Yeah, hopefully," Seethan said. Then he addressed the black shape in front of him. "How can we be sure you can be trusted?"

"Because now we're under the protection of the Seelie and – as we said – we want to make amends as best we can."

"Do you…have a name?" Eve asked.

When the creature demurred by shrugging its shoulders, Shipman said brightly, "Then we need to give it one. What about Chovy? Proper military nickname."

"It isn't military," Eve said.

"Excuse me?" Shipman replied, with raised eyebrows. "Look at it this way, he was used as a weapon by our enemies. And, if you think about it, ants are militaristic in nature. Surely that speaks for itself."

"Agreed," the commodore said.

"But why Chovy?"

Shipman snickered. "Well, we have nicknames like Bomber Mills, Jumper Cross, Sux Cox. Had a friend who had an aged stripper as a girlfriend. Her name was Rabone, we called her Thrower. It took one guy called Hunt six months to figure out why he was nicknamed *Isaac*. And this fella's name's Chovy because he's–"

"Yes, we get it," Eve said, interrupting him. "As in Anchovy. Now, are we going or what?"

*****

As Seethan had previously noted, autumn was definitely upon them now. It was as if Van Gogh had been set loose upon the landscape, painting the trees with leaves of gold, red, orange, and browns in a stunning explosion of colour. Perhaps it was a final and defiant shout at nature, before the snows of winter descended upon the world. That dampness assailed the nostrils and filled Seethan's bones and joints with dull aches. He couldn't help but wonder how his many transformations had affected his joints. From his current aches he knew he'd be paying for those in time. Had he been a super hero, he mused, he'd have been called *Captain Concrete*.

He'd seen murmurations of Starlings in recent weeks, the birds weaving complicated cloud patterns amidst the evening skies. Intermittent flocks of duck, swan, and geese passed overhead with a varied loud cacophony. Robins became far more noticeable, remaining in place while other breeds of birds fled to warmer climes. Fawns and calves could be spotted more easily, as the leaves began to fall and carpet the ground in their rustling and swirling glory. Seethan wondered how much longer it would be before the deer began to shed their antlers, as they always did as winter approached. As the days progressed their rutting subsided, their grunts and deep throated belches diminishing as they clashed less with the passing of the season. The group walked on, Eve occasionally bringing down the occasional fowl with her bow or catching fish while they camped overnight. Seethan himself added to the menu by hunting prey while in wolf form.

On the third evening they stopped next to a slow-moving river, to top up their water bottles. Sometime earlier in the day Eve had skewered several fat-looking rabbits with her arrows and, along with Shona, skinned and cleaned them as the others set up the camp and fetched fallen wood for the fire. Chovy drained away and reformed into a face upon a nearby, quite wide tree trunk. Said face was easily three times the size of a normal persons, and it gazed upwards, watching with shiny black unblinking eyes as the smoke was whisked skywards in thin grey tendrils. Clouds hung overhead like a thick furry blanket and – while no stars could be seen – the pale luminescence of the moon shone through the clouds as if fighting to keep watch over them.

The colonials had each brought with them a package that literally sprang open to form a two-man tent and the only thing now needed was to peg them to the ground. They shared one of them, leaving Seethan and the two ladies the second. To Seethan, the interesting thing about the tents was that somehow they blended into their background no matter what it was – thus adding to their security. Thankfully, this also meant they no longer needed to spend time and effort creating make-shift shelters each night, or risk wet weather by sleeping under the open skies. Now, all they had to do was get a fire going.

Seethan could smell rain even when it was some distance away. Now, he sensed an oppressive storm approaching. Thankfully it hadn't taken them long to make camp, and now he set about securing a peaked canopy high enough above the fire so that it wouldn't be scorched or otherwise damaged by the heat. The canopy would protect against downfalls, but there was always water that swept in sideways, like waves from the sea thrashing a beach road.

"There's a storm's coming," Seethan advised the others as he worked. "A nasty one. We need to collect what firewood we can while it's still dry, and then find a way to keep it that way. I suggest we store some of it in our tents, to use as and when needed. I don't know how long the wet weather will last, but I fear it could be a while."

"How can you smell rain?" Shipman asked, brown eyes widening in surprise.

"How do you think? I'm a werewolf remember. We have a strong sense of smell, and can even pick up the aroma of unwashed bodies and clothes from some distance away. Except yours, that is. Why is that?"

"I'm an officer of the Colonial Forces, and I tend to wash regularly rather than stink up the place, apparently unlike marines. Surely you must remember when you had those values. It's only a suggestion but maybe you should think about stripping off and taking a shower in this coming deluge of yours."

Seethan gave him a feral grin. "Touché."

Even as Seethan spoke, there came the pitter-patter of rain hitting their surrounds. Without a word everyone swept out to collect firewood, before it was too late.

There was a sudden loud cymbal of thunder.

"Okay, so you were right about the weather," the commodore said, ditching an armful of wood under the canopy and then lifting his hands over his head as he groaned and stretched.

"I would be, if you think about it. All of my senses are heightened." Seethan counted seconds between the tempestuous drumbeats. "The storm is getting nearer." Even as he spoke there came clash of thunder, followed almost immediately by a flash of light as forked lightning danced overhead. The tempo of rain increased, its impact becoming hard enough to sting. Seeing Andrews' ample stack of wood under the awning, the others dumped their armfuls within the confines of their tents. Thankfully each of them had waterproofs of varied sorts, which they quickly donned. It protected their attire but then, as expected, the rain found its way into their hoods. The cold liquid slid down inside and leaked into the clothes underneath, chilling them further, and they shivered despite the fire. The ladies handed out plates of steaming food, and Shipman looked down at his with a puzzled expression.

"What the hell is this?"

"Prairie chicken and beans," Seethan answered dryly. At the other man's raised eyebrows, he then added, "Or to you, rabbit."

Shipman watched each of the others eating for a moment before risking a bite. His expression changed and he chewed thoughtfully for a while, before saying, "Hey, this isn't bad. I wonder if we can get this stuff added to our normal rations. It would certainly break up the monotony."

"People used to breed bunnies to eat on the colonies when I was serving," Seethan said. "Mainly the new start up projects. You know, where there wasn't much food and so forth. Luckily, they bred quickly. But they usually escaped and bred like wildfire. I guess all that would have been some time back, to you."

The weather worsened. Each of them, apart from the one on watch, took to their tents to wait it out. Thankfully the now battering downpour and increasing wind didn't rip the tents free from sodden ground. A spring-loaded clip in each peg released spikes that drove sideways to help hold them tight. It was only when those clips were eventually released that the spikes withdrew back into their housing, and the pegs could be pulled free.

The storm was unrelenting. They took it in turns at sentry duty, under the awning while also tending the fire. Normally when they rested Chovy often dissolved into columns of ants, which had initially streamed away to find food. But, to their surprise, this time he soon returned and told them that he also needed shelter from the inclement weather, or his colony would be at risk of drowning in the downpour. Two streams of ants, many bearing eggs, marched into both tents where they reformed into much smaller versions of himself and settled down in a corner. Seethan lay down opposite Chovy, suddenly much more aware of a strange smell, something like vinegar coming from the ants. Despite that, he made room for Shona and they all soon drifted off to sleep.

Eve shook Seethan for his watch sometime after midnight. Gently rocking him she leant close, her mouth next to his ear and whispered, "Seethan, stop sleeping! You're on watch. Come on, I've made you some tea."

Her hands lingering on his chest and her warm breath in his ear brought thoughts and urges he wished they didn't. It's been a long time since Rose had died, and his wolfish romps with Fey were also in the past. He was embarrassed of his increased sensitivity to Eve's scent and the way she had deliberately brushed her breasts against him as she spoke in his ear. He already sensed that she had feelings for him, and he felt an almost uncontrollable urge to take her up on the obvious offer.

But he couldn't.

Life was difficult enough. He still loved Rose and, no matter how he felt, he wouldn't betray her again – even though she was long gone. Oddly, he wondered what Rose would have thought of his current situation. Would she advise him to take up Eve's advances, or prefer him not to? Mumbling his thanks Seethan sat up and Eve drew away. He couldn't see her eyes but knew that, again, they'd be filled with disappointment. Shona lay silent but he didn't think Eve cared about what the witch saw or heard or, in fact, care about what anyone thought.

It was weird being in there with the ant man, and it took a lot of trust, knowing that it had devoured those villagers. That Shona was only gradually gaining her powers back was little comfort and he doubted she would be of much help if things went pear-shaped. What would happen if the Unseelie managed to regain control of Chovy? Would The Golden Ones be able to step in and prevent carnage once again? Finally, he shrugged and thought, well *you've gotta die sometime, right?* Although he could think of far better ways to go than being eaten alive by ants.

Eve opened the flap and left the tent. The rain beat against the fabric like peas poured onto a metal plate; it was unrelenting. Donning his waterproofs, Seethan took a deep breath and stepped out into the downpour. Luckily the fire was only a few steps away, but by the time he got there his head and shoulders were already soaked, his chest and back drenched despite the hood.

Eve smiled as he arrived and handed him a steaming cup. It was coffee! Thanks heavens for the two colonial officers, who were more than happy to share their supplies. There was even sugar and whitener, which he stirred in. He sat next to Eve on a rotting log that had been pulled up earlier to serve as a seat of sorts.

"Thanks, I certainly needed this. Nothing going on to worry about?"

"Not a thing," Eve replied tiredly. "I'd say it's as quiet as a mouse, but with the rain coming down like this that would be a lie. At least the thunder and lightning has stopped."

Seethan looked into her brown eyes as she gazed at him. Thankfully, over the long months, she'd forgiven him for allowing her brother Chris to be turned into a werewolf. For a long time, she'd barely spoken to Seethan, even though it had been her who had begged for them to do it. Seethan had been unable, knowing the consequences, but Andy had stepped in. At last, it seemed, she'd come to grips with it, and with the monster her brother had become. As if reading his mind, she spoke suddenly.

"Have you seen Chris of late? He said he'd pop in now and again."

"I smelled that he'd checked us out briefly a short time ago, but the pack are far away now. Don't worry, I imagine he'll come calling when they eventually get back. He's a man of his word and probably didn't want to disturb you at a late hour during his last visit. You could try asking Shona to call him with her mind." He could do that himself, but he steered away from it.

"And what is she supposed to say, *here boy*?"

Seethan ignored the barbed comment and said, "Well, she's getting her powers back slowly and surely. Hopefully she'll get them back fully quite soon. I've a horrible feeling that we're going to need them."

"Me too," Eve said sulkily. "Guess I better go get some shut eye, although I can't see this storm abating for a while. We might as well take the opportunity to rest up, rather than any risk. In this weather Chovy won't be able to walk with us anyhow."

"Aye," Seethan replied. "Go get some sleep, you look like you need it."

She hesitated, and then blurted, "Seethan, once you've finished your watch and have dried off, you're welcome to share my furs. They'll be warm and yours cold. It's just an offer, think about it."

He smiled gently. "Thank you, but I'll be fine. I'd hate to bite you in my sleep. You wouldn't be happy if you woke up as a puppy, now would you."

She looked like she was going to say something more but then changed her mind. Her face hardened and, turning away, she walked back to their tent, shutting the flap securely against the foul night.

*****

Three days later the rain stopped, leaving them a swampy mess. Thankfully the area they'd chosen for a camp was raised higher than many of the others around them, which had flooded due to burst banks from the bloated waterway.

Realising that they had to traverse the river to continue their journey, and that it had swollen to a point where its flow was more of a rush, they decided to wait for a while before crossing, and despite taking the opportunity to scout for a safer place to cross could find none.

On the fourth morning Seethan knew now was the time. The levels had dropped and the pace of the now brownish river had slowed considerably. Putting on his backpack and using a pole to feel his way, Seethan slowly crossed the river – chest deep in places, even more so in others. Luckily, with the aid of the pole, he found a fairly safe route, pulling a line behind him. Despite his best efforts the water had pushed him downstream somewhat, but at least the way he'd found was safe. Confident that all was well, the others gathered their packs – with large balls of ants balancing atop each of them – and also made their way across the shushing waters. They had to keep going back for more of the ants, as they just couldn't carry enough between them and many had been left behind.

Shipman had collected the last of Chovy and was on his way back when he was engulfed in a huge splash and totally disappeared. A few moments later he resurfaced, battling a huge croc that had hold of one of his arms. Seethan knew that these beasts had been moved around the planet by the Spooks, and it was the second time he'd personally seen such an attack. The first had been many moons ago against a villain in the New Forest; having been snatched from the shoreline the man had never been seen again. Despite the fact the man had been a killer, Seethan would never wish such a death on anybody. In fact, it brought a shudder to him each time he thought about it. Shipman, however, was battling against the gator like a demon possessed. With a cry of almost primal rage he thrust his thumbs into the beast's eyes and ground them in.

At the unexpected, and no doubt agonising, counter attack the croc let go of the man and Shipman quickly splashed his way to the shore, helped to safety by them all as they plunged into the water to rescue him. Once ashore he retched, spewing forth spurts of murky water and chunks of debris. The ants atop his head had sadly been washed away.

"Are you okay, Lieutenant?" Andrews asked, slapping the man on the back in an effort to quell his coughs.

"I'm good, thank you Sir." Shipman finally spluttered. "Please stop."

Seethan stared at the man in disbelief. By all rights he should be dead, how could he survive after being attacked by such a monster as that? The beast had been easily around five-metres in length, probably more. As the man settled down, he asked him outright.

Still coughing somewhat, Shipman said, "Those things are on other worlds too you know. People shipped them to farm for their skins and for meat, of course. Full of protein, low in crap. We were taught how to defend against them where I was enlisted, told to go for their eyes. They tend to release you quite quickly then. Luckily, I had one arm free and was able to do just that. But the last thing I expected was to be attacked by an ocean-going handbag, I hope the damned thing's blind in one eye now."

"But, your arm," Seethan insisted. "It should be broken if not bitten off, but it looks like you're having no problems with it. How's that?"

Shipman looked at Seethan as if he was daft and rolled back the sleeve of his uniform, to display a greyish garment underneath.

"What is that? Looks like some kind of body armour?"

"Exactly, but a relatively new version that diplomats have had available for some time. It's been a few years since our last meeting, Seethan, and things have changed," Andrews said. "The military tend to stick with coloured external armour, as it also works as a visual deterrent. I thought it prudent we wear this version instead of the other, particularly as this is really a diplomatic mission." He rolled up his own sleeve to show his own.

"How does it work?"

"Organically. It's filmy, so you hardly notice you're wearing it. If someone takes a pot shot at you, though, it reacts instantly and stiffens enough to stop most weapons – including teeth, it seems."

Shipman was continuing to massage his arm with a pained expression. "This stuff's good but it still hurts like a bitch."

"Just imagine how you'd feel if you weren't wearing it," Seethan said. "Your arm would either be crushed or ripped off. I'd be thankful, if I were you. As it stands, it's only your love life that's going to suffer."

"Funny!"

"Do you want me to take a look at your arm?" Shona asked, her face wrinkled in concern.

"No thanks, it's nothing serious. Just a bit of bruising, which matches my ego at the moment."

The ants had snaked away from the packs and Chovy reformed, silently watching them all with those black expressionless eyes. He didn't even mention the thousands of his nest lost in the river such a short time ago.

They moved on in short order. The river bank was bordered by a muddy rise on both sides. Thick grey tree roots stuck out haphazardly, like a senseless ladder. As well as being soaked through they were all covered in mud by the time they got to the top of the rise. They paused to refresh themselves and put on some fresh clothes, before shouldering their packs and carrying on once more.

As they walked Seethan asked himself, what if the croc hadn't attacked? Would he ever have found out about the armour? If things had gone awry with the Spooks when these guys arrived that personal protection could have worked badly against him and the locals. Especially if arrows were unable to penetrate it. At least he now knew that only head shots would have any chance of success, if needed. He wondered what else they weren't telling him. Call him suspicious, but this exposed secret made him question everything he knew about the two colonials and his trust in them slipped somewhat.

The journey was hard going. They followed the track of the river, but the ground was boggy and sucked at their boots, making a pleasant afternoon's walk into a gruelling trudge where they often had to drag their feet free. As they walked along the edge of the river Seethan noticed something. A barely noticeable long dark shape following them just under the surface.

"Everyone, move away from the edge!" he said. "The croc is following us. I can see its head just there, under the surface. Get back, now!"

"I didn't know that they bore a grudge," Shona said, edging away from the river.

"Nor did I," Seethan said. Then more urgently, "Come on, Eve, move!"

He quickly reached out for her hand, just as the ground underneath her collapsed and she toppled backwards towards the water. He grabbed her barely in time, and tried to yank her towards him as hard as he could, even as the others rushed to help. Seethan still clutched her hand but was unable to do much more. Somehow, he felt weak and disorientated, his head splitting with pain. What the hell was wrong with him? He tried to transform in a desperate bid to gain the extra strength needed to pull Eve towards him, but nothing happened – something was stopping him. He felt as if he were being torn apart, the strength leaving his body as if it were being funnelled away, while the screams and images of past battles filled his mind.

The giant croc erupted from the water and snapped at Eve. Only Shipman grabbing hold of her at the last minute saved her life, as he wrenched the young woman from the water. The huge jaws missed by millimetres. With a huge splash the reptile landed in the shallows, soaking them yet again. Then, with a huge swirl, it swam away and disappeared beneath the murky surface.

"Seethan, what the hell?" Shipman said, looking at him in astonishment.

"Never mind," Shona said. "Help me, quickly!"

She grabbed Seethan and put his arm around her neck so that she could semi-carry him, the Commodore immediately doing the same on the other side. Between them the two dragged him a short distance away, where he began to recover his strength and his breathing began to slow.

"Damn!" Seethan spat, shaking his head in an effort to clear it.

"Look," Shona said, pointing back towards several clumps of waist-high plants. They were tipped with a multitude of purple flowers, shaped like cowls, clustering at the top of tall and thick green stems, like blackfly infesting a nasturtium.

"Devil's Helmet," she added. "Also known as Wolfsbane. It's extremely poisonous and in normal conditions weakens all lycanthropes. I thought you'd have known about that by now, Seethan."

"I do," he gasped. "But I didn't see it. I'd have smelled it, if my nose hadn't been dulled by the stench of that water. Even if I had, what else could I do?"

"Thank you," Eve said, returning to hug him tightly. Then she faced the river. "We need to come back here and kill that thing. It's not only feeding on humans, it's actively hunting them. We need to warn people about it."

"Too right," Shipman agreed. "I'll be having bloody nightmares about that thing for ages."

When Seethan had fully gotten his breath back, they set off again. Finally, they stopped on a rocky outpost, where they could watch their surrounds with ease. But it wasn't an ideal spot to pitch camp, and it was too early. They had several hours of daylight left and so they moved off once again. Chovy retained his perch upon their packs. Thankfully, the ants didn't weigh much and so the group didn't mind. Better that than risk possible drownings. At dusk they reached the outskirts of a village.

"This is it," Chovy said, leaving the packs and reforming itself. "The village we told you about."

They group glanced uneasily at their companions as they entered the village. It was eerily quiet, not even broken by birdsong. It wasn't long before they began to pass bones, easily recognisable as that of adults and children as well as animals and fowl. Seethan could make out the remains of dogs, cows, pigs, chickens and what looked like ducks. But it was the children that really got to him. If Chovy was telling the truth and it had been forced to do this, then the Unseelie had a lot to answer for. But there were always two sides to a story, and he knew that they had only heard the ants' version of events. What if this was all some kind of elaborate trap?

Chovy stopped, his black eyes peering sightlessly at Seethan. "You have to understand that this is how we live in terms of hunting for food. We would never have done so willingly against humans, for with your intelligence we almost see you as kin. We also understand the concept of loss and are truly sorry for what has happened. This act must be avenged – by you humans for your loss, and by our people for being forced into such an act."

Somehow Seethan found those soulless black eyes haunting. Chovy hadn't quite mastered the art yet, for one eye moved independently of the other. The creature's shape was definitely based on a male; weirdly standing there naked, a living effigy right down to his fingernails and manhood. Even his muscles bunched and then relaxed as he moved.

"We need to bury these people," Seethan said.

"Why?" asked Chovy.

"Because that's what we do."

"In which case, I'll help. I killed them; I will dig the hole."

That's odd, one moment he says 'we' and the next 'I'. Wonder what the hell is going on in that strange, alien mind of his. Then he said, "Very well. We'll stand well away so that we don't injure any of you underfoot. We'll gather the bodies. There's already a graveyard over there," Seethan pointed to one corner of the village. "Let's use that."

In a very human way Chovy nodded and strode over to the burial site, where he disassembled into his millions of members. Seethan and the others searched through the buildings after clearing the streets, laying the bones they found on rugs or in sacking that they collected from the dwellings. It took them well into the afternoon but by the time they'd finished collecting the bodies Chovy had also finished digging the hole. He reconstituted himself and stood looking down into it, in which Seethan and the others laid the villagers to rest one by one. Seethan lost count of how many there were, and it was almost dusk when they finally began filling the hole back up.

At the end of it, each stood a while in silent contemplation, before returning to the dwelling they'd selected to stay the night in. Meanwhile, Chovy remained standing beside the grave, solemnly looking down with his hands crossed.

"What's he doing?" Eve asked, as they turned before entering their thatched, stone cottage.

"Thinking ant things, I guess," Seethan replied. "And I can't even begin to imagine what they might be."

Chapter 7

They left the silent village early next morning. As still as the grave, one might say. There wasn't any birdsong to be heard, no farmyard animals call, nor even the shuffling and scampering of nervous rodents, shriek of an owl or of other critters in the undergrowth. During the previous night the silence had been somehow threatening. Shivers ran up their spines, as if they were being watched by something unseen. But when Seethan took his turn on guard duty, he had used all his senses to reach out into the darkness and had detected nothing. No spectral feet trod those empty paths, no evil or sinister eyes stared back at him from something unimaginable hidden within the darkness.

He was glad to be out of the village, his wolf-enhanced eyes constantly scanning, nose twitching. Eve walked silently besides him along the endless tracks, arrows on her hip yet bow ready in her hand – just in case something for lunch presented itself. They passed previously well-tended crops in fields that would now turn to ruin. As they came across penned cattle and fowl they freed them, so that they could fend for themselves.

Seethan had noticed in recent months that she'd started wearing a home-made lemongrass scent. She was good at making perfumes, he knew, and sold them to villages near to what they now called home. He'd watched as she peeled the lemongrass stalks before grinding them with mortar and pestle, adding a carrier oil and mixing well. She would leave the concoctions out in the sun for several days before straining and restraining the liquid until it was clear. Of them all, that lemongrass was his favourite. Not that he told her. It wasn't exactly slap-around the face strong, but it held a mild yet bitter hint of lemon that seemed to dance back and forth across his nasal pallet. A clean and welcoming smell. She'd taken up the art after he'd told her that Rose wore a scent of orange blossom, and how much he'd liked it. He couldn't help but wonder if it was because of him, or she'd simply taken it as an idea for a small cottage industry. As an android, Rose's body could exude such scents at will. Eve's took much more effort, and he was grateful that she hadn't attempted the orange blossom that would remind him too much of his former lover. Instead, she had created something that was distinctly her – along with several others. Her market, he knew, had been growing; her perfumes becoming sought after amongst those who came across it.

Seethan's feet crunched through dry, fallen leaves that carpeted the ground with rusty-gold and other autumn colours. The air now held the acid touch of winter, an icy sharpness that made your nose tingle. As he breathed in it brought back a flashback to the first time he'd been injured in a firefight.

One moment he was walking along a pleasant country path, the next he wasn't. Memories, smells, sounds, and feelings from the past were vividly relived. He could reach out and touch long-dead friends, even shake their hands and laugh with them.

From time-to-time aircrew were used to make up the numbers, usually when the craft they piloted became non-operational. When that happened, the pilots were just other marines. During that mission his ship had landed easily enough but a malfunction that prevented take off again had flashed up almost instantly. Unfortunately, despite their abilities, it couldn't be repaired on site and so Seethan and his co-pilot had grabbed their weapons and joined the troops readying for the next part of the mission.

He'd been a first lieutenant back then. The unit took heavy casualties during an assault on a nest of pirates, who'd been plaguing in particular the large container ships mundanely coasting between far colonies. The marines had taken cover in a shallow depression in the ground, partially shielded by dark-green foliage that snapped aside and flew into the air as projectiles shredded them and dug into the musty-smelling mud. They knew there were bound to be snipers in the trees. He could almost taste their presence, his guts clenching in response as his eyes scanned for a betraying movement or heat signature. A sergeant called in air support and soon white trails of incoming missiles lanced down from the sky and plunged into the enemy positions. The brilliant rosebuds of explosions, the boom of intense noise making him blink despite his experience.

A voice called out suddenly, "Hit the deck, hit the deck!"

The command came from everywhere at once and Seethan slammed into the soft reeking ground, but even as he embraced the mire there was a sudden hammer-like blow to his foot and a feeling of numbness that quickly spread up his leg.

"Stand to, platoon Bravo advance. Alpha, covering fire!"

Seethan tried to stand up and return to the machine gun that hurled small but powerful armour-piercing explosive rounds at the enemy. He couldn't. Something was wrong, what was it? He looked up at his sergeant.

"Hey Sarge, I can't stand up. Why the hell can't I stand up?"

The weathered marine had calmly reloaded his weapon before looking down at him. Pushing his helmet a little higher with one grimy forefinger he said with a feral grin, "Because you've been shot, you twat..."

He came back to the present; those now distant memories so clear in his mind. Thankfully the wound hadn't been too serious and he'd healed quickly, only to discover that it wasn't an enemy bullet that had got him but a round from his own side. As designed, his combat boots had compressed his foot and so kept it in one piece. Everyone had found it extremely funny at the time, except for him of course.

Bastards.

Shona spoke to him suddenly, breaking the spell. "We should be there in a couple of days, it's not that far really."

"As the crow flies," Andrews said, as Red skimmed through the autumn trees ahead and then back around them, alert for danger that could come in so many guises.

Seethan focused, listening to faint sound of dry leaves being crushed underfoot. Other leaves rustled and danced in that never-ending wind that brushed like an unseen spirit blowing gently against his cheek. The temperature was much cooler now, bordering on cold.

They crossed the many streams that barred their way, most fairly shallow and others not, meaning they had to go upstream to find an easy way to navigate them. Once again, they had to swim across the chilled waters of a somewhat deep and fast-flowing river, using ropes to ensure they weren't swept away.

Shipman was their strongest swimmer and so, with a rope around his waist, he'd gone first. Once on the other side he'd anchored the rope around the bole of a tree and pulled from the other side of it, helping the others across. They'd all made it safely, their so-called waterproofs were completely soaked through; all bar the two colonials whose clothes repelled the water and kept them fairly dry. Seethan had worn similar garments in times past, but his one remaining tattered and torn uniform was now reserved for special occasions – even though his discharge from the military had been confirmed by Commodore Andrews many years back. Once at a safe distance from any waterborne threats, they stripped, dried off, and then changed their clothes, building a fire to dry the rest out. Given the time they decided to make camp for the night, which thankfully passed smoothly. Early the next day they'd set off again.

Around mid-morning they came across another gateway, this one resembling a shimmering waterfall tumbling noiselessly across the path ahead of them. They passed through it without thought and found themselves in a deep valley with walls of trees rising steeply around them. Seethan suspected that they weren't that far from their previous location – at the most a hundred miles or so. Later in the day they breached another gateway and found themselves on a grassy plain looking towards a fort that had a wooden-wall of sorts in the distance. Behind that citadel the trees continued on to stretch back as far as the eye could see. The vale itself looked as though a giant had slammed a massive axe into the countryside, leaving raw stone cliffs – the ravaged sides of which rose to a considerable height on either side of them.

The cut bled gradually into a wide meadow. Long grasses surrounded the citadel as they approached, while besides them a wide muddy-coloured river giggled manically. They soon came across and began to follow a well-trodden man-made ash path that lay in relatively good order. Waist-high beige grass, the tops of which were fat with seed, rippled in the wind as if brushed by a giant hand, creating a rushing sound like that of muffled deep conversation.

"At least we'll be safe and in the warm tonight, rather than sleeping on this bloody hard ground." Shipman said in his posh baritone voice, as they approached the fort.

"What's up, too used to hotels?" Seethan inquired with a half-smile.

"Bloody marines!" Shipman retorted. "You think the rest of us live a life of luxury. It's far from it."

Seethan noticed Shona and Eve giving them both concerned looks and he chuckled, before saying, "Don't worry, it's only banter. Taking the mick out of other parts of the military is something we naturally do. There's never any harm intended."

Both ladies looked to Shipman, whose nod and answering grin put them at ease.

Before long they'd reached the rectangular outskirts of the settlement, in the middle of which lay a tall gate. Towers lanced towards the sky from either side of the entrance and corners of the fortress, all connected by imposing wooden walls that had spikes atop them. In all his time here Seethan had never seen defences like this, and he wondered what it was that they were so afraid of. The fortifications were all rough-hewn and apparently untreated wood.

To be truly effective those walls should have been made from stone, which meant that either the occupants were short on time or lacked the equipment. A more concerning development were the three rows of strong-looking wooden spikes, each as long as his arm, set one in front of another with only a small gap between them. Most were dug securely into the ground but here and there they were embedded in heavy blocks of wood. All of them were only a few paces in front of the walls. Seethan felt a chill run through him, something was very wrong here.

Chovy stopped suddenly and turned to them, "I'm sorry but I can't enter the village."

"Why the hell not?" Seethan asked.

"They may know about the villagers I killed and be afraid of me. I also don't want to take the risk of it reoccurring." Chovy added that his memories of the event were still raw, and that he'd rejoin them when they finally left the establishment.

"It's all right for us to risk it on a daily basis though," grumbled Shipman.

A horn sounded and echoed around them, no doubt coming from one of the lookout towers. Within minutes locals dressed in leggings and rough belted shirts of various colours came out to greet them, gesturing for them to stop where they were by holding their palms up and shouting at them. They then pulled a small section of the board-mounted spikes to one side, and pushed an odd-looking wooden bridge through the gap that remained. With the aid of a wheeled mechanism of sorts they swung it out towards Seethan and the others, and only when it had clumped into position did the villagers call and gesture for the group to come forward.

The bridge was solid and wide enough for six people to walk abreast of each other, no doubt designed to allow the passage of carts and perhaps cattle for trading purposes. In a few moments Seethan and the others were across and facing the villagers, all of whom looked somewhat trepidatious. One of them, a pock-faced grizzled fellow who looked like he shaved with a chipping hammer, swaggered forward and faced them, hands on hip.

"I'm Olaf, leader of our council of elders, welcome to the village. How can we help you?" He looked pointedly at their unbulky packs, "Doesn't look like you're you here to trade. It's been a very long time since we had visitors, so we're pleased to see you."

"I'm Seethan and this is Andrews and Shipman, our friends Eve and Shona. These men are from the Colonies, the Spooks let them through to talk. In fact, we're on our way to see them now."

That raised eyebrows, and a mumble of subdued conversation burst out amongst the villagers.

"Now why would they do that?" one of them asked more loudly. "The Spooks don't allow colonials here, everyone knows that. The last time they did there was that awful battle. This could be some sort of trap."

"Things have changed since the last time we were here," Andrews said. "There are much bigger threats than you know."

"Tell me, what's with the bridge?' Seethan asked, changing the subject.

"We just crossed a covered moat," the local said, gesturing at the ground on either side of the temporary walkway. "Trust me, you don't want to fall into it."

There was a rumbling sound and they all turned to see the bridge being swung behind them, and pulled back to its former position. The three rows of stakes were carefully replaced where they had been before, leaving no gap in the defences. Just before Seethan and the others passed through the open double gateway there was a carved wooden sign bearing the name, *New Haven*. Once inside the fort, the heavy doors creaked closed behind them.

They found themselves in a quaint town with buildings of various heights and design, some wooden while others were stone-built. Oddly, there were dwellings underground, as if they had been dug to protect the citizens when all else failed. At the entrances of each were rockfalls that could be triggered by those inside to seal the doorways when needed.

Sound swelled from a market street laid with a cobblestone road. Along each side were rows of what looked like apartments, shops, and occasional cottages. There was quite a bit of greenery all around, which Seethan found surprising. It was as if the inhabitants, while they enjoyed their security from the surrounding countryside, still longed for it. To him it appeared that the fortress walls had been built around the village, not the usual way in which a village was squeezed into the limited space provided.

Olaf led them down what appeared to be the main street, which consisted mostly of shops. Here and there were several floors of rentable apartments, and a few bars. Numerous people stopped to stare at them as they passed, obviously unused to visitors. Arriving outside an Inn with s sign that declared, '*The Hole in the Wall*' they entered the open door and took seats at a large rectangular table atop greyish rough-hewn flagstone. Ensuring that they were comfortable, Olaf ordered drinks.

"So, you're from the colonies?" Olaf said to Andrews and Shipman, as he seated himself.

"They are." Seethan said, interjecting and answering for them. "As I mentioned earlier, they came to talk with the Spooks. But first, if you don't mind me asking, what is it with these fortifications? I've not seen anything like them since I've been here and if we're in danger we'd like to know about it."

Before Oaf could reply, a buxom barmaid with a low-cut top bent over to deliver them each wooden beakers of ale. Seethan found himself unable to avert his eyes from the view, and the young raven-haired beauty gave him a knowing wink. He found himself blushing. But, then, she gave the same response to the commodore.

"We're being haunted by a tyger," Olaf said, oblivious to the byplay. "It appeared out of nowhere a year or so ago and started stalking the inhabitants of our town.

We've never had anything like it around here before, so not only was it hard to believe at first but that disbelief cost us lives."

"You said it was a tyger?" Shipman said.

"Aye, you could say that we have a very big cat problem," said Olaf, noticing the man's confusion.

"Well, surely it can't be that hard to deal with. Why don't you put down some kitty litter or something, and stab it while it's having a crap?"

Seethan stared at Shipman, trying to determine whether the man was serious or dense. Then he turned to Andrews and said pointedly, "You know, sometimes I really do wish our pistols worked here. You can't cure stupid but you can shoot it."

It didn't seem to register with Shipman, who next suggested, "What about kibble?"

"Lieutenant, unless you have something intelligent to say – which I sincerely doubt," the commodore said, "I suggest you remain silent. Olaf, I'm sorry about my friend, please excuse the interruption and pray continue."

Olaf looked from one to the other and then gestured to an older bearded gentleman who sat in one corner smoking a thick, white, wide-bowled and smooth clay pipe. With the aid of a walking stick the fellow ambled over and joined them. He accepted a mug of beer from Olaf, pulled the pipe from his mouth and sipped at his drink with obvious pleasure. Olaf introduced the fellow as Peters, their village Chronicler. The elder asked the man to tell them all they knew about the creature that was plaguing them.

Peters replaced the pipe in his mouth, drew in deeply, and breathed out a thick cloud of pungent grey smoke, the acrid smell of which Seethan found somehow pleasing. The man began his tale with how the fairy folk used to visit the village in the dead of night, and seek out gems that had been hidden from them. Apparently. The practice had turned over time into more of a game than anything, enjoyed by both parties. The story rang a bell in Seethan's mind, similar as it was to the one Shona had told them. This had to be the actual village the story originated from.

The chronicler continued to tell them how it was also profitable, as the fairies left nuggets of gold in payment for what they took. In a rough grumbling voice, Peters added, "It was a good arrangement even if it was unofficial and a bit lop-sided, sometimes the gems were worth a lot more than we received back in payment, while at others our reward was the greater. It's as if they didn't understand what value was. The Fey, after all, had the ability to easily work the stones into jewellery. Their skills are far greater than ours, and we had nowhere else really to sell them, without undertaking long journeys – which we dislike."

"So, what happened? Because something obviously did," Seethan said.

"Indeed. There was a ruction in the Fairy ranks over some of the stones and who should have them. A fairy by the name of Willow came and told us this, when she was passing through here after being banished from their realm. She said that the Fey had split into two factions, the Seelie and the Unseelie – or Fairy and Faery. The latter were led by the Queen's twin sister, Mab, who blamed the whole thing on us, as it was here that the stones originated.

"As a result, Mab and the Unseelie cursed our village and sent the tyger to punish us. The creature is vile; it bites its victims' necks to choke or paralyse them before dragging them away into the countryside."

"Have you actually seen this beast?" Seethan queried.

"Hell yeah."

"What does it look like?" Seethan asked.

"It's big, mean as hell, and bloody fast too. It's Tan-coloured, which allows the damn thing to merge with the grasses around the village. That means it can appear from where you least expect it. What's more, the creature is exceptionally smart and it can jump a surprising distance and height," Peters replied.

"Why do you call it a tyger, if you've never seen one before?" Seethan asked, a frown on his face.

"Because we found a poem about it in our library," Olaf replied.

Seethan knew that many settlements had a library of sorts, perhaps consisting only of a few frayed books that survivors of the invasion had managed to take with them as they fled. A last link, perhaps, to their past. In many of those villages' efforts were being made to keep the art of reading and writing alive. Unfortunately, it was becoming a dying art.

Peters closed his eyes and recited the poem from memory. His rough voice filling the hushed room with subdued menace.

"Tyger tyger, burning bright,
In the forests of the night;
What immortal hand or eye,
Could frame thy fearful symmetry?

In what distant deeps or skies.
Burnt the fire of thine eyes?
On what wings dare he aspire?
What the hand, dare seize the fire?

And what shoulder, & what art,
Could twist the sinews of thy heart?
And when thy heart began to beat,
What dread hand? & what dread feet?

What the hammer? what the chain,
In what furnace was thy brain?
What the anvil? what dread grasp.
Dare its deadly terrors clasp?"

"I'm sure there must have been more to the poem," Olaf added. "But the only bit we found was on a tattered half-page in a sorry-looking book. Luckily, those who discovered it could actually read and they saved it, rather than use it as kindling. Above the poem was a drawing of a creature that looked very much like the beast that had been stalking us – although that one has stripes and ours has not. It's a giant tawny-coloured cat, with teeth more like daggers than anything else."

"I saw a tiger once," Seethan said. "In an off-world wildlife sanctuary that was attempting to keep several creatures from extinction. It was awesome, huge, easily came to my chest height and was longer than I am tall. Not the sort of thing that you easily forget."

Peters explained that the tyger generally hunted in the silent hours, so residents were forbidden to leave the safety of the village in the dark. But, that said, it had also been known to hunt during daylight.

"We didn't have time to mine stone to create a proper fortress, so we did what we could and built the barricades from wood – to provide at least some form of defence. But even that took time and we lost people while doing so. And when the fortifications *were* erected, the damned thing treated them with contempt and just ran up the bloody walls, as if it were a normal cat climbing a tree. I shit you not!

"We then built the towers to give us more warning, before digging the dry moat which we laced with spears. You'd think that would be enough, wouldn't you? But the beast was somehow able to sense it. Would you believe it jumped right over the moat, climbed the walls and caught another victim? Out of desperation we put down our third measure, those rows of spikes you can see in front of our walls to stop it jumping over – adding some pointing downward at the top of the barricades to try and deter the beast, just in case."

"But why a dry moat?" Andrews asked. "Cats can't swim and you could divert water from the river easily enough to fill it up."

"If only it were that easy. You see, unfortunately you're wrong; this bugger *can* swim. It was seen swimming across the river over yonder."

"Getting scoffed by that thing must be a horrific way to peg it," Shipman said.

Seethan and the others just looked at the man and then carried on, ignoring him completely.

"We had to think again," Peters continued, "got rid of the pathways and burnt down the long grasses that it uses for cover. We have a portable bridge now, that we can shuffle about from time to time, to stop the creature from anticipating where we might cross next."

"That would be enough to deter anyone," Shipman said.

"That's an understatement." As Olaf spoke, silence fell in the room, the other patrons looked pensive and worried as they listened in. He wiped a greasy hand on his dark-tan leather jerkin and took another sip of his drink, his wizened face crinkling in appreciation.

Seethan looked at Olaf. "I take it you've tried hunting this thing?"

"Of course we did; twice actually. But it simply tore the hunters to pieces, I'll never forget those screams. We gave up after that, due to an understandable lack of volunteers. Like Peters said, the damn thing's smart."

"Andrews looked into his cup and said, "Do you have anything stronger than this stuff, whisky or rum perhaps?" He smiled as a gesture from Olaf brought the waitress over with a beaker full of God knows what. He tried it, grimaced, and then he said, "What about trapping this animal?"

"Apart from hoping it would fall into the moat, you mean? Well, we dug other pits here and there but they didn't work either. Creature must have a sixth sense or something."

"Don't you have anyone with the Craft here? Perhaps they could help somehow. Mask the scent of the traps for example, that might be useful." Shona asked.

"Craft? You mean as in witches?" Olaf snorted. "The ones that were here took off when it became clear who'd sent the beast. Didn't want to cross the Fey, they said."

"A baited trapdoor might do it." Andrews continued. He stared down into his mug and took a sip, shuddered, and then took another.

Olaf blinked, and then said, "Come again?"

"A baited cage with a trapdoor that slams shut behind

the creature once it enters," Seethan said. "I've used them in the past, not for tygers mind you. The creatures I was after were much smaller but really nasty with it. The principle is the same, though. The first thing you need to do is figure out how big the cage has to be to hold it yet restrain too much movement; and what strong enough material you have available to make it from. And then, of course, there's the question of bait."

"Bait?" Olaf said, raising a thick and unkempt eyebrow.

"What about using Shipman?" Seethan suggested.

Shipman blinked, staring in disbelief at Seethan while the commodore and Olaf smirked but said nothing. Olaf ordered more drinks, which arrived along with a few nuts and pastries that were filled with a lightly-spiced mixture of aromatic vegetables.

Olaf informed the barmaid that rooms were needed for their guests. As soon as she had gone to sort it out, Andrews turned to Shipman and said, "You've been acting a bit odd since we got here. Are you all right?"

"Yes, sorry Sir. I have some kind of headache. Had it since orbit, actually. Guess I should have had it checked out before we left the *Aurora*."

"Yes, you bloody well should have!" Andrews snapped. "If this mission goes pear-shaped because of you, I'll make those days you spent in a military prison seem like a holiday! For heaven's sake, focus man. Get a grip, a lot depends on this."

"I will, Sir. My apologies."

Ignoring the verbal jousting Olaf said, "I warn you, that cat is mean and pure muscle. This cage you mention can't be made out of wood, because I'm fairly sure it could easily smash its way out. We need something much stronger, metal perhaps. Trouble is, there isn't a lot of that lying around."

"What about making it from stone?" a voice asked from the background.

Olaf shook his head and replied loudly, "Don't be daft man, how the hell are we going to move something like that once it's built? We need to be able to get out there and then back as quickly as we can, people's lives are at stake."

"Well, we passed some bamboo on the way here. That stuff's really thick and strong, I guess we could use that." Shipman said.

"Bamboo's wood," Andrews said. "Olaf said it won't be strong enough."

"No Sir, it's a type of grass believe it or not, and it's surprisingly strong."

"Grass?" Andrews' said, looking surprised, but he didn't argue.

"Well, how far is it from here?" Olaf asked.

"A couple of miles at the most, that-a-way." Andrews said, pointing back the way they'd come.

"Ah, I think I know where you mean. The trouble, of course, is harvesting it. Not going to be easy, as I've no doubt the tyger will be out there waiting for us."

*****

During the night Andrews used rough hand-made paper and charcoal supplied by the villagers to work out that they needed a cage around four metres in length, three metres wide and about the same high. Early the next day, after a good night's rest, Seethan and his team – along with a large armed group of locals numbering sixty or so, led by Olaf – made their way to where the bamboo grew.

On the way, Olaf told them about the previous hunting groups. It turned out that each had only held a total of four men. Andrews told him that was nowhere near enough to discourage such a creature from attacking, although it would no doubt whet its appetite. With luck, the number of armed and deliberately noisy people they had now should help deter the creature.

They took with them donkey-pulled carts, one loaded with spare weapons, water and food, while the others were empty and ready for their crop. They reached the site safely and it didn't take long for them to start work.

Soon the spare wagons were filled with lengths of wrist-thick bamboo and the worker's mood lifted somewhat. Each time the wagons carried their loads back to the village they were escorted by twenty or more determined and well-armed locals.

All the time they were out there, Seethan had the distinct feeling that they were being watched. His hackles rose and his wolf instincts screamed at him. However, he wasn't foolish enough to transform and go out there to try and find the creature. He was supernatural, not stupid.

Even the commodore commented on the sense of being scrutinised, and the group as a whole became concerned once more, convinced that the tyger was just waiting for an opportunity to strike. That prospect never arose. When they'd finished the entire party arrived back at the village safely, much to everyone's relief. The carts creaked worryingly from their heavy loads, and even the mules looked exhausted.

Once back in the fortress, Shipman and the commodore started work on the cage, with Seethan and others pitching in once they'd seen how to do so. The villagers had an ample supply of a strong hemp twine, which they used to secure the struts of the cage as they built it. To everyone's surprise the contraption was completed in no time at all.

Between each bamboo strut was a space of equal width, with two rows of bamboo secured vertically on the outside to strengthen it. A drop-door complete with four largish bells was attached and tested, to see if people could hear it. Several of them, in turn, played the part of the beast by entering the trap and – once sprung – trying to see if they could batter their way out. None of them could. The drop-door itself worked brilliantly, the bells loud enough to be heard back in the village – which is exactly what they wanted. The bells themselves were cumbersome and heavy enough not to be disturbed by the constant wind, and so there was little risk of a false alarm.

Or so they hoped.

Using further struts of bamboo underneath to lift it, only four men were needed to carry the cage over the bridge to where they'd decided the best place to put it would be. They then laid the contraption in the grass, which had now regrown to almost Seethan's waist. Said grass was quickly woven between the bars, which not only effectively helped mask it but made the trap look more inviting, like a cool shelter and a great place to hide. It was hardly noticeable during the day and practically invisible at night. They hoped the meat they hung up would be enough to entice the animal. The leg joints of a poor unfortunate goat were heavily laced with a sedative that Shona had devised, in the hope it would knock the creature out and suffer less. The witch then spent a few moments mumbling over the trap, stating that – with her improving powers – she was dispelling the scent of mankind.

Checking it the next day revealed a dead fox, which had apparently tried out the bait and overdosed on the medication. This left the villagers no choice but to use live prey, rather than risk other scavengers needlessly. Hopefully, the scent and constant bleating of the bait would draw their quarry. Seethan felt for the goat, but knew there was little option. He found himself sitting down opposite the scruffy black and white creature, apologising and explaining to it that while none of them wanted it to suffer the villagers thought that it was better to sacrifice one animal than risk losing more of their friends. He doubted, however, that the goat saw it from their perspective. None-the-less, he felt awful. He never felt guilty about hunting when it was for food, but to sacrifice an animal like this felt wrong.

As darkness fell on the second night, Seethan's team took turns keeping company in the towers with the villagers, but nothing untoward happened. Nor did it on the third night. The fourth, however, was completely different.

*****

It had turned midnight and all was quiet except the distant, haunting hoot of an owl accompanying the goat's faint bleating. The moon cast its eldritch glow over the surrounding countryside, showing the grasslands rolling like waves in that ever-present but gentle wind. Seethan's eyes were constantly drawn to the stars above them which glinted like chips of ice.

He remembered deployments to distant colonies during his time in the Marines, but that had been well before the Sundering. Seethan's jaw clenched involuntarily as he thought back to that day. He and Rose had taken off on their fateful attempt to rewrite history even as the Spooks descended on the Earth. They'd tried to engage the invaders; tried to do anything. But their boss had remotely commandeered their ship, and initiated the time-jump in atmosphere. The next thing Seethan knew, he was waking alone in the forest, marooned in the far future beside a vast crater. One, it turned out, their explosive departure had caused. The sight of it still haunted him.

A shooting star blazed overhead and caught his eye. He watched its brief trail across the sky before it suddenly fizzled out. Clear as they were now, the skies had been heavily polluted back in his own time, forcing the World Government to reduce emissions as much as they could. To help with this they had ensured citizens used the hover-bus services, by heavily increasing the associated costs of private vehicles until only the very rich could afford them. Seethan had been lucky; driving in the military had still been classified as a necessary skill and so part of his training.

*****

A sudden clang of bells broke the silence. It was accompanied by bellowing roars as the trap went off and the creature within it went berserk. The villagers were roused by the uproar and soon a very large crowd had formed, with some climbing up onto the battlements in hope of seeing what was going on, while others thronged the towers. At the start of this venture, it had been agreed by all that should the trap be spring, they'd wait until daybreak before investigating. This way should the creature break free it would be long gone by the time they got there. If not, it would hopefully be safely restrained and exhausted by its attempts to escape.

It wasn't long until morning, so none of them returned to their beds. Instead, they made drinks of hot herbal tea and chatted, each of them evidently seeking the reassurance of their comrades that the creature had at last been captured – and that they would all survive to see another day.

*****

Finally, it was time.

The hunting party made their way over the bridge and towards the trap, from which the mind-bending screams of animal outrage had eventually ceased. All of them cast concerned looks into the surrounding grasses as they went, crowding closer to each other as if they thought that by doing so would save them from any attack.

When they got to the trap Seethan was stunned by what lay inside. The tawny creature within the cage was massive and simply oozed threat. Rage-filled golden eyes glared at them through the bamboo struts, as it spat and hissed through a chainsaw mouth. But what really took his breath away were the long bayonet-like teeth that curved downwards to a point below the bottom jaw. Tremendous muscles rippled without a hint of fat, as it tried to spring at the cage. But, cramped as it was, the tyger had no room to do so.

Suddenly the big cat roared. It was so loud that many clasped their ears, some simply dropped their weapons and fled – leaving only those with the staunchest of hearts behind them.

When the bellows of fury had died down, Olaf said, "We need to somehow carry this whole contraption back to the village, rather than trying to subdue and tie the beast up out here."

"That's irony for you," someone said. "We spend all this time trying to keep the bugger out, then we capture it and carry the damn thing in."

There were a few other comments and snorts of amusement, before Seethan said, "Umm, that cage is going to be damn heavy. It will take quite a few people, what with the change-overs of those carrying it needed. Let's face it, that's one solid-looking critter. And what are you going to do with it once you get it there?"

"Kill it, what do you think? It should be done in front of the whole village, so that they can witness it and be unafraid from then on." Olaf glared through the cage at the tyger, his face pulled back in a grim, hungry, and satisfied smile. When he spoke next it was as if he were addressing the tyger directly. "Do you think that I'm scared of you, Kitty?" Reaching carefully behind the creature he thrust a hand between the bars and touched the cats skin. "Incredible, feels this like solid oak. Such power and...ow, ow! For fuck's sake!" He snatched back his hand and clutched at his wrist, his face twisted with agony.

"Even I wouldn't have been that stupid." Someone behind them said. "Fancy putting your hand in a tyger's cage. For goodness sake!"

Olaf had pulled back his left hand to display rivers of blood streaming from slashes all down his forearm. They looked deep, but he held the wounds tightly against his body and muffled his moans. With a murderous expression he lifted his spear with his good arm and thrust it straight into the creature's side. It gave a deafening roar of pain and exploded into action, twisting and turning, those golden eyes flashing with the promise of death as it slashed at the cage holding it. And then, quite suddenly, it keeled over and lay still. Olaf thrust the spear into it again and again, burying the weapon deep into the motionless body. The spear was soon joined by dozens of others, leaving the big cat's body an oozing mass of spikey flesh. Blood gushed from the open wounds and sprayed briefly from its mouth and dripped out of the cage. It was a sad end to the magnificent creature.

Any words of protest from Seethan were bitten back as he watched the weapons being thrust home. While he understood the feeling of relief the villagers must be having, he felt that the ignoble death of such a beautiful animal was tragic.

Eventually the cage was lifted with the creature's body still inside and carried all the way back to the village walls, where it was extracted and displayed lengthways between poles for all to see, in front of the gate. Never in his life had Seethan imagined he'd be witness to such a sight. Even he couldn't resist in joining the others running his hand down the cooling, rough-furred and bloody hide.

The delighted citizens soon began celebrating in style. A dance was held in the village square. Drums and flute music filled the air, tables had been moved aside allowing more space than normal. Vendors cooked enticing food with scents that made one's mouth water. Andrews was quickly partnered with a well-put-together dark-haired lady called Molly, who had a ready smile and great sense of humour. To Seethan's surprise the couple disappeared early, taking their celebrations elsewhere.

As the night drew on eventually only Seethan and Shipman remained of their party. The others, apart from Andrews, had one-by-one retired for the night. Lost in his thoughts Seethan was surprised when the lieutenant arose from his seat on the other side of their glowing brazier and came and sat next to him. He shuffled closer, until their legs were touching.

"You okay?" Shipman asked, his eyes warm and quizzical.

"Fine, why?"

"You seemed a little withdrawn, and I wondered if you'd like some company tonight."

Seethan took a deep breath, stunned at how the

suggestion had come out of nowhere. "Erm…no. Thanks for the offer but I'm totally straight."

Shipman sighed and a slight smile played over his lips. "Ah well, you can't blame a fellow for trying now can you. But let's keep this to ourselves, if you don't mind. Each to their own I know, but I like to keep my life as private as possible."

Seethan nodded, before slapping the other on the shoulder and saying, "Yeah, no problem. I just don't get why you made such a fuss about my shorts now."

Shipman snorted, and poured him another drink, their conversation turning to military banter.

*****

In the early morning there was a huge commotion. Seethan and the others woke and raced outside to see a great many of the villagers bearing shocked and terrified expressions, more than a few having armed themselves. Seethan could immediately see why.

The body of the tyger was missing.

Chapter 8

Once the discovery was made known, Olaf called a town meeting and grabbed a chair from outside a bar. Standing on it and cupping his hands in front of his face so that those at the back could hear him, he bellowed, "Who's responsible for this, who took the tyger's body? Speak up, damn you!"

Peters ambled forward leaning heavily on his gnarled walking stick, pipe jutting from his mouth from which those constant clouds of fragrant smoke wafted. He tucked the stick under one arm and brushed aside his white hair, before saying loudly, "I am." He stood there defiant, hand on his hip and unafraid, in front of his friend.

"What the hell do you think you're doing?" Olaf demanded.

"Done, actually. That creature was pure evil and you know it. We didn't want that carcass bringing bad luck to the village, so we got rid of it by dumping the body into the ravine before someone came up with the daft idea of cat curry."

"Are you mad?" Olaf demanded, spittle flying from his mouth. "Yes, I'm pretty sure it was evil but it would have made a fine exhibition piece once stuffed. It would have drawn visitors from all over, and brought in much-needed income! You've cost this village a fortune, Peters. Damn you man! You two," he gestured to a pair of men in the crowd, "come with me. Let's go and get it back."

"Sod that, I'm not going," the two men echoed.

Someone else said, "Hell no. If it's dead, leave it be."

"You won't find the carcase anyway," Peters said. "We flung it far into the middle and the beast fell into the deepest part of the ravine. We didn't even hear it land. If you want to climb down there, be my guest. Whoever does that needs to be a far braver man than I and, to be honest, if you do find anything it will be pieces of flesh scattered all over by the impact. It won't be much good to anyone."

Olaf's jaw tightened in anger, his arms bulging with muscles. Fists clenching, he snarled. "You're a bloody fool Peters. Get out of my sight, all of you." He jumped from the chair, turned and kicked it back towards the bar from where he'd gotten it, and then stomped off fuming.

Seethan hid a smile while Olaf was creating merry hell. He suspected that Olaf had actually wanted the hide for himself, maybe for a wall hanging or coat. A chance to brag to visitors and strangers. But fear is a tangible thing, and the people had been terrified. From listening to those around him it appeared that the ravine was dangerously deep, and was to be avoided at all costs due to the sheer drop and crumbling walls. He was advised that several people had lost their lives trying to climb down into it over the years.

Olaf stamped about all morning, grumbling and shouting at those who got in his way. His left arm was heavily swathed in bandages, from which blood still leaked. His blistering tirade at those responsible for the theft had gone on for what seemed like hours and Seethan doubted it would stop soon.

Seethan and the others decided to remain in the village for a day or two longer; they could all do with the rest, and a chance to replenish their stores. When he eventually calmed down, Olaf promised the travellers whatever they needed as thanks for helping remove the threat. Come mid-morning the village had unanimously voted it a holiday, and everyone was in a jolly mood. By mid-afternoon the bars were crammed with people and numerous barbeques, spitting hot fat from various meats, were set up in the town centre. Seethan participated in an archery competition, plus knife, spear, and axe throwing. It was a lovely thing to see everyone so relaxed and thoroughly enjoying themselves, after recently being plagued by such horror.

The party continued into the night and a dance was held in the clearing on the far side of the bridge, outside the settlement. Tables had been set up out in the warm, clear night. Some tables had rough coverings of cloth or woven grass. These were quickly covered with ale and wine, slices of bread, meats, salads, and even chunks of hog roast and water fowl. The welcoming smell was enough to make anyone salivate and the clamour was unbelievable. It was as if the populace, once so subdued, now delighted in venting their freedom.

Seethan found Eve staring at him and asked her what was wrong.

"It must be nice to have heightened senses – to be able to hear, smell and see all kinds of things that most of us can't."

"Not always," he replied. "It's a gift, that comes at a cost."

Just then there was a shriek out in the wavering grass.

"What kind of animal was that?!" Eve demanded.

"The one with two backs," Seethan replied with a smile. "Some things you just don't want to hear."

In the middle of the partying Eve suddenly leapt to her feet. "Something just crawled over my foot," she said, shoving her chair away from the table. "I think it's a scorpion. I hate them. Damned lucky it didn't sting me, that would have really hurt."

"Seriously?" Seethan asked incredulously. "We have scorpions here now?"

"Yup, bloody nasty ones too. Been in this part of the world for years. I've kind of got used to them, but that doesn't mean I have to like it. They give me the creeps."

"A bit like me with spiders," Seethan answered. "Here, I'll check it out for you."

"Let me help," Andrews said, dropping besides him.

They lifted the woven grass table cloth and slipped underneath. Seethan led the way on his hands and knees, holding a candle in front of him. He couldn't see much. Peering into the shadowy areas he edged his way forward. Maybe it was hidden in the cloth, where it touched the floor and lay in folds. The irony was that he hated spiders, but had just remembered that scorpions belonged to the arachnid family. He shuddered, but carried on.

"Maybe it was a mouse," Seethan finally said, seeing nothing. Breathing out a sigh of relief he started to withdraw. As he did so he heard sniggering from Shipman.

"What's up with you?" he said, as he returned to his seat.

Shipman sniggered again and held up a piece of melon. "I was going to drop this down the back of your neck."

"I'd probably have knocked you the fuck out," Seethan replied, not seeing the humorous side at first. Then he gave way to a grin and, he too, chuckled.

Andrews had paired up again with Molly from the night before, and he was soon lost in the crowd during a slow dance. She had told them earlier that she worked as a barmaid at a local tavern. Dark haired, slim waisted, sporting a stunning chest made evident by low-cut tops, she was staggeringly beautiful. Seethan couldn't help but wonder where this was going, and if this would all lead to heartbreak. He hoped not, the commodore was a good man and he deserved a break. He was staring into his beer, morbidly thinking about Rose, when suddenly there was a terrified scream, as a large tawny shape slipped into their midst from the surrounding grassland. Muscles rippled beneath that ochre hide, the paws about twenty centimetres – if not more – padded into the very middle of the crowd.

It was the tyger. Somehow, it was back.

But this time the monster was dead. Everyone could tell, for its rheumy and cold eyes stared unblinking at them, and savage wounds that didn't bleed gaped in the creatures' sides. Its stomach and chest had been torn open, so that ribbons of flesh dragged at the ground. Without warning it threw back its head and uttered a roar that was hideous beyond belief, forcing everyone to cover their ears as they fled. Luckily there were armed guards still around, but not as many as there might have been. Spears were launched and impacted the creature until it had a dozen or so jutting from its torn body like quills from a porcupine. The big cat just shook itself lazily, as if they didn't exist, and pounced at one of the guards.

The man's scream of despair and agony was cut short as the tyger bit off his head in one fearful mouthful and then spat it aside. Without warning it then lay down with its paw over the body and began feeding. A few of the guards held onto their spears, which they thrust in turn at the beast as they dared to approach it. Horribly, chewed pieces of human flesh had started to fall from the creature's open gut onto the ground beneath it.

"For God's sake get back," Seethan shouted. "You can't kill something that's already fucking dead!"

"This can't be!" Peters said in disbelief. "We threw the damn thing into the canyon. Nothing could have survived that; I saw it with my own eyes!"

"Well then, I guess that must have royally pissed it off," Seethan snarled, shouting again for everyone to retreat back into the village. To his surprise Peters was well ahead of him in the rush. Was he putting his physical struggles on, or did the beast from hell give him some added impetus? Seethan didn't care, but guessed that all Peters wanted or needed to do was beat him through the gates.

Seethan had taken his eyes off the beast for just a few seconds, as he too ran, and then he heard Molly scream. He stopped and spun around to see the big cat darting towards her fleeing form.

In seconds Seethan's clothes had shredded and he'd transitioned into the wolf. The brute in him intercepted the big cat just as it caught up with Molly and leapt at her. Seethan bowled full pelt into the side of the tyger, knocking it over even as those jaws stretched out for her. Both creatures landed in a whirling snarl of fur, teeth, claws, and fury. Molly pulled herself to the relative safety of one side, her eyes wide with terror.

The big cat clamoured wearily to its feet and turned those lifeless eyes on Seethan, one of which now hung loose from the socket. That eye swung back and forth like a grim pendulum, until it finally came free and tumbled to the ground. The beast didn't seem to notice, it just leapt at Seethan who nimbly danced to one side, his front paws slashing at the tyger as it passed him, ripping one of the creature's forelegs free.

It landed heavily, collapsing on one side. Seethan was besides it in a second, ripping at and breaking first one and then both of the rear legs. The big cat lay on its side, the one working limb still swiping at him, even as Seethan kept out of range. When the wolf in Seethan moved it was so fast none of the witnesses even saw it, only the cat's usable limb being tossed away like a fallen branch. Villagers armed with axes charged at the corpse and began hacking at it. In moments all that remain was a mess of stinking, decomposing flesh and bone.

"Throw it on the fire!" Olaf commanded, and as the villagers complied the acrid stench of burning meat soon competed with that of putrefaction. Then the village elder turned to look at Seethan, who had swiftly changed back into human form and stood there naked next to his pile of discarded and torn clothes, as if suddenly unsure what to do. He said nothing for several moments, as slowly many of the spears turned to point towards him.

"So, you are one of the cursed," Olaf said, at last. "You must know that the damned are banned from all villages, and yet here you stand soiling ours with your presence."

"Just as well he was," Shipman interjected loudly. "This man saved all your lives."

Olaf paused and thought for a moment, and then responded slowly. "Yes, he did. But everyone knows that werewolves can't be trusted, they easily turn on their friends and family. I cannot risk that in our community, our women and children are here."

"We've been here days," Andrews growled, "and nothing happened. If Seethan had wanted to attack you I'm sure he would have by now."

"Exactly," Seethan said. "The only reason lycanthropes turn on those they love is out of despair. They're left to fend for themselves, to live or die on their own. Not all lycanthropes are bad, we're just badly misunderstood. Something that's happened throughout history, just think about the elves."

"Indeed," Eve said. "But then, they're often their own worst enemy." Looking up she began to sing. She had a lovely voice, and Seethan had heard her perform the song before, though he'd never really paid much attention to the words. It reminded him, somehow, of stories he'd read when he was young - long ago, now. He wasn't the only one taken in, it seemed; Olaf had lapsed into a stunned silence, and other villagers were listening spellbound.

Elven arrows in my heart
I know it cannot be
For she is out of legend
And I am only me

Our villagers fear these ancient woods
And the hunt through which it rides
Each time we hear those ghostly horns
They all just run and hide

Don't go into the woods, they said
Yet I could not ignore these glades
Where rivers run clear and the water sings
Before vanishing 'neath trees' shade

There is a magic to this place
You can almost hear it call
You can see it in another's face
In their expression most of all

I run between these tall proud trees
Through rivers clear and chill
I can hear the humming honeybees
As they buzz the flowers' frills

Nectar, how it scents the air
Old leaves, that earthly smell
Then I hear the horses' hooves
And see faces, grim and fell

With armour so brightly shining
Whilst pennants flutter atop their lances
For home I won't be pining
If I can but attend their eerie dances

Majestic horses' snuff and snort
With heads held up with pride
Know they're not the common sort
For legend they have astride

These ghostly knights
How tall, how proud and brave
Some would find it a ghastly sight
And it would lead them to their grave

These silver ranks, at last they part
Haughty there stands the queen
With startling deep-blue eyes
And skin a snowy sheen

Raising a hand to me she points
Then finger crooks and she smiles
The music starts and a horse produced
And I ride with them for miles

A forest rescuer's whistle sounds, "come to me!"
Yet far too late, this attempt to even start
Why should I wish it, can't they see?
For there are elven arrows in my heart

"The elves protect these forests," Seethan said "And they'll do so at any cost. There's a lot of strange things out there, these days, and werewolves are just another.

Many are dangerous, but that's because they can't control themselves like I can."

Olaf sighed heavily. "I'm sorry Seethan, but you're cursed – you have to leave our village. We daren't risk you staying here and I *have* to think of my people's safety. I'm sorry, but I'd like you gone by morning."

A muttering grew around them and swelled rapidly into loud protests, as the spears were lowered and shouts of support for Seethan grew, until Olaf finally gave in.

"What the hell is the matter with you lot? This is what we've always done," Olaf said dismally. "Well fine, he can leave the day after tomorrow then, but if anything happens in the meantime this is on all of your heads. If he gets hungry during the night and attacks someone, don't blame me. I, for one, will be barring my doors."

"I can control the transformations," Seethan said, giving him a pleading look. "And what's more, I've been teaching others how to do the same. With luck, it will change people's outlook on lycanthropes. If you really don't mind, I think we'll stay a little longer."

"And how the hell are we supposed to tell the difference between those of you who can control it, and those that can't?" Olaf snapped. "Where's Peters? That man is supposed to be second in charge, he should be helping."

"Last time I saw him he was doing billy big steps into the village. I think he was winning our race earlier, incidentally," Seethan replied, with a smile.

*****

Seethan went to see Olaf, to discuss their arrangements and departure. He was met at the man's front door by his sister, a tall and slim woman with long black hair and brown eyes. It looked as if she had been crying, for her eyes were red and puffy and she held a white hanky to her nose, sniffing slightly.

"I'm sorry," she said. "He's gone hunting. Said he'll probably be a couple of days."

"Oh. Are you okay?"

"Yes, I'm fine. What is it that you wanted?"

"I only want to talk to him about my group's plans. Who did he go hunting with?"

"Just himself."

"Isn't that usual?" Seethan asked.

"Not really, but he's been a bit out of sorts since that tyger-skin episode. He feels threatened by people ignoring his wishes, and wants some quiet time. Look, there's only he and I left in our family now. Dad died years ago and the tyger got our mother some time back. I know Olaf's a bit grumpy at times but he's a softy really at heart. All he wants is to do the best for everyone and it frustrates him when people don't see things his way. Please, think about that and be nice if you see him."

"I will, don't worry," Seethan said with a kindly smile. He turned and left, walking slowly down the path towards the square, his mind in neutral. For once the village was relatively quiet, until a young lad of about eight years of age came running up to him.

"Sir! Please, can you come with me?"

"Why?"

"Peters sent me to find you. He says it's important."

"Okay," Seethan said with a sigh, casting away the image of a steak pie that he'd had in mind from a local shop. He followed the lad through the city gates and outside through the barricades. After crossing the bridge, he came across Peters and two others standing still and looking at the ground.

"What's up?" Seethan asked, as he joined them.

"Look," Peters replied, pointing towards a large paw-print on the ground. "That's the tyger, if I'm not mistaken."

"Hardly a surprise, since it was here during the party – before we chopped the damned thing into mincemeat and burnt it. What's the problem?"

Peters said nothing but pointed to the long grass on his left.

Seethan saw that where Peters was pointing the grass

was trampled, and there was something else. Confused he walked over and stared. Before him, half-hidden was the body of an animal, although it was a tad difficult to tell exactly what it was. In the few remains scattered about the bones had been crunched into red-stained dagger-like shards. Feeling his mouth go dry, he turned to Peters and said, "And?"

"Well, don't you see? We both know that's the work of a tyger, and I'm pretty sure this wasn't here yesterday. Nor was that print."

"But you're not certain?"

"Not one-hundred-percent. This site was a hell of a mess yesterday and I had the villagers clean it all up. I even inspected it afterwards."

"Why?"

"Part of my job as a village elder," Peters said indignantly, frowning over the top of his pipe, "is to ensure everything remains tidy and that there are no problems that might deter people from coming to our village. You're not dense man, think it through. I'm pretty sure our big cat is back."

Seethan looked at him, considering. "You aren't serious. That thing was burnt to ashes and everyone saw it. There's no way it could ever come back, and if it did all it could do was make people cough. Have you discussed this with Olaf?"

"No, but I will."

"Good. In the meantime, let's not panic. We don't know for certain there's another big cat out there. By the way, if you're so convinced about that why are you standing here with no weapons or guards?"

Peters jerked and looked startled. "Hell, I hadn't thought of that. We only just found this. Come on guys, let's get back inside."

*****

The streets that had earlier been filled with jubilant villagers were now only haunted by shadows, the glare of the gibbous moon lighting the main street and slim back alleys with subdued light. Music could be heard from within a few abodes as Seethan passed them, along with voices talking and laughing.

Somewhere a dog barked repeatedly. It was strange, as he hadn't seen one of the animals since arriving. Perhaps, at last, they finally felt safe enough to announce their presence. Carrying a spear Seethan walked out of the huge gates, hearing them shut firmly behind them. He carried on walking until he got to the river, drawn by its cool music. Olaf was there, as Seethan knew he would be, staring out over the water glimmering in the moonlight. He sat down beside him.

"Are you okay?"

"Yes," Olaf said gruffly. "Why?"

"Peters is saying there might be another tyger."

"There isn't one. The daft old sod just missed seeing those prints previously."

"You sound pretty convinced," Seethan said, laying down his spear. "Not interested in the chance of another skin?" He offered the man a flask of wine.

The elder glared initially but then said, "Thanks, I could do with a drop. I think if there had been another beast we'd have seen or heard it by now. It would also have attacked the villagers that have been going back and forth cleaning up that damned mess."

Seethan accepted the flask and took a sip himself. "You don't need to say anything. I already know."

"About what?" Olaf turned to glare at him but then, when Seethan didn't answer for a bit, he slumped and said, "How?"

"Let's just say that I get a sense about these things. Besides, you gave in far too easily at the village when you said you were going to throw me out. It made me curious and I couldn't figure out why, but then it came to me. I didn't believe it at first, but my senses told me the truth, and then I remembered how the tyger clawed your arm. After our visit from the zombie tyger I figured that maybe the Dark Ones had learned a lesson or two from the Spooks. I'll also bet that those scars on your arm are fully healed now. You're just hiding them under that bandage. I'm right, aren't I?"

Olaf gave a long sigh. "You say that you can control it. Do you think you can teach me how to do that?" His eyes now looked like golden orbs with black lemon-shaped centres as they reflected the moonlight.

"I can try. It's really down to each person, how much you want it and so forth. Come on, let's get away from here and we'll get started. The last thing your people need is a feline version of me."

Chapter 9

Come morning and Olaf sent out word that he wanted a meeting of all villagers in the square. The word went around quite quickly and, as the crowd grew, Olaf pulled a chair from the tavern closest and stood on it, calmly facing the throng. He quietened their questions with two downward-palm-motions, waiting patiently for those around him to be quiet.

At length he cleared his voice and said, "Our guests have decided that it's time for them to continue their journey. But, we ourselves have gone through hell. Because of this, I feel it's important for one of us to represent our village in the talks with the Fae, and to join these people in their quest. But, if anyone should go, it should be me as your leader. Therefore, I will be leaving with them. Hopefully I'll return in the not-too-distant future."

"But, you're our elder," someone shouted. "It should be someone else that goes."

"Someone much younger!" another shouted.

Olaf looked affronted at the latter. His rugged face twisted as he spoke, "Yes, I'm leader of the elders and so it should be me. They'll recognise my authority and, in the meantime, I'm nominating Peters to stand in my place. He'll do the job well, particularly as he suddenly seems to recovered some of his fitness..."

His words were met with laughter as Peters stepped out of the crowd. He stopped and leant heavily on his stick. His ever-present pipe puffed like a miniature volcano. He actually managed to look indignant, "I thank the ancients that the tyger gave me the strength and ability to flee. I believe our ancestors called it adrenalin, and I know that I'll pay for it later. But Olaf's right, that's the fastest I've moved in many moons. I begin to feel it now though, it's as if I've been run over by a herd of cows. But no matter, at least I'm alive – and so are the rest of you.

"So what, the tyger's gone for now. But what if they send another? We can't let our guard down until we know for certain this is all over. Olaf's right. He's our leader and has the authority to represent us." He turned to his friend, "The position of village elder will be waiting for you on your return. In the meantime, I'll look after it. Our thoughts and prayers go with you."

*****

Seethan hadn't told Shipman and the others what was going on with Olaf, but knew he had to. He waited until they were several days away from the village, and had made their first camp in the evening, before doing so. It was Olaf, standing beside him, who told them in person.

"Well, that's a new one on me," Shona said, after a moment's silence and wincing as she sipped a cup of hot herbal tea. "I've never seen it myself but I have heard of such in legends."

"Ailunthropy is the feline version of the lycanthrope, which as we know is the werewolf. Both are forms of therianthropy – which is the ability of humans to transform into animals," Shipman said suddenly.

The others looked at him in surprise.

"What? I have an eidetic memory. It's how come I got selected for the military."

"Well, thinking about it, that makes sense," Seethan said. "It's well known that those with high IQ's don't often have common dog-fuck. And, for you non-military types, that means they've no common sense."

"There are so many different types of these creatures," Shipman continued. "For instance, a berserker is a werebear, while–"

"Okay, stop," Seethan said, "We get the picture."

Shona was looking at Shipman in surprise. "I've actually learned something from you. Perhaps we should talk more often."

"I wouldn't," Seethan replied. "Unless you want your brain turned to jelly. Too late for Shipman, though, obviously. What did you do, read encyclopaedias as a child?"

Shipman, big as he was, managed to look hurt, but said nothing in reply.

Shona said to Olaf, "So, this change, is it an involuntary thing, like with the wolves?"

"Yes. But Seethan says he might be able to help me. Hence the real reason for my joining your group. The last thing I want is to be cast out from my village and into the wilderness. But I'd rather that than risk injury – or worse – to anyone else."

"You're the first elder I know of who's willingly put themselves into such a situation," Seethan said. "Perhaps you can help make people see that we can be a help rather than a burden. After all, what bunch of marauding warriors would attack if they knew a village might have these…creatures…in it?"

"A good argument," Olaf said. "I'll remember that, thanks."

"So why don't you two go out and hunt for something to eat, or are you going to sit there and growl at each other all night?" Eve said with the hint of a smile.

"I can't just make myself change and go off hunting when I want," Olaf said. "It's an involuntary thing that only happens during the full moon. The weird thing was, I kind of sensed it was going to happen before it did. Hence why I went out on my own previously."

"With the Unseelie learning all the time," Shona said, holding up one palm and studying a small ball of brilliant-blue energy hovering above her hand, from which sparks of electricity flew. "I'm not surprise that they discovered the Spooks ability to instil transformations into people. I also suspect they'll be coming up with many more tricks to scare the shit out of us. Now, go get us something to eat."

Seethan rose and gestured for Olaf to follow him. The latter stood, glanced at the others, and shadowed his new friend into the gathering dusk and the rising moon.

*****

Olaf spent every free moment talking to Seethan and studying the PTSD tools and strategies that he shared. Most nights the two would disappear together and not return until sunrise.

For Seethan the transformations hadn't been easy, but he'd long experience with controlling his PTSD; with practice, it had translated into controlling lycanthropy. Olaf, however, needed to learn it all before he could begin to apply it. But then again, so had the rest of the pack, and they'd eventually mastered what they needed. Olaf, unfortunately, struggled. On the first night of hunting together it had been Seethan who finally transformed and brought back a deer. For a while Olaf only managed to change during the full of the moon, and that was more involuntary than anything. Seethan remained hopeful though, because he knew that Olaf sensed what was about to happen during the moon and took himself far enough away to not cause anyone harm. Things developed over time, and Olaf gradually learned the skills he would need to transform as and when he wanted.

For the team, while Olaf studied, trees weren't a viable form of escape should he come calling, for they all knew that the original tyger had been able to climb New Haven's walls with ease. Consequently, when Olaf was out alone during the full moon the others sought the safety of a cave, or hollow. Otherwise, it meant clustering in the open in one group with two or more standing guard, spears at the ready.

As powerful as he was, Seethan knew he was no match for a tyger, let alone a were-tyger. He was outmatched and knew it. But none-the-less, when Olaf was out alone, he transformed when necessary and took his turn patrolling the camp.

It was a week or so later that they come across a village that was apparently unthreatened. Short of victuals, they decided to visit it and top up their supplies. There was no problem with that, for both Andrews and Shipman had brought with them some gold coins – a centuries-old survival strategy for military specialists going into theatres of combat or threat. It didn't matter that the coins were in colonial currency, for gold was gold and it was the weight and purity that truly mattered. It easily transferred into almost all currencies, no matter where.

Having filled their needs, they decided to stay overnight at one of the inns. Oddly, it was named 'Shaggy', and its hanging sign was that of a large dog – which, after laughing, Seethan took for a good omen. They looked forward to a warm bed for the night, and a hot meal that they didn't need to hunt and cook for. Seethan still had a few of his own coins but kept mum about the fact. He knew that he might need them one day. With luck, the two visiting colonial officers would soon fulfil their mission and be gone. Let them spend their own coins in the meantime.

It was Eve who had booked the rooms, the only five that were available. The commodore had his own single room, as did Seethan, Olaf, and Shipman. Eve and Shona shared the only available double. Chovy, as per, remained hidden outside. It was as if he'd developed a fear of humans and other races discovering what he'd done, that they might then seek revenge. Seethan and the others had tried talking to him, to let him know that he had nothing to fear. But it was to no avail. Seethan wondered how many childish pranks and experiments had added to that fear over the centuries. He'd been told that children had once found it amusing to burn ants with magnifying glasses. If so, it wasn't in his time, and he abhorred even the thought of it.

Dinner was a wonderful steak-and-kidney pie, along with mashed potatoes, carrots, broccoli and gravy. It was followed by oven baked-apples and cream, the combination of which had fully sated their appetites. A pint or two of the tangy but strong local cider finished off the evening. It was the usual cloudy and strong-tasting form, that had unnameable bits floating around in it. As a child Seethan had been told it was bits of mice and so forth; whether that were true or not he didn't know, but mused that another saying – 'that it was akin to drinking a hand grenade' – *was* indeed the case. A few jars of the brew later they were succumbing to tiredness and made their way, one by one, up to their rooms. After such a long and exhausting journey so far, they were all looking forward to an early night and a comfy bed.

It was late when a gentle knock on his door awoke Seethan. The werewolf in him sprang awake instantly. Grabbing his knife and gripping it fiercely he slipped silently to the door. Standing well to one side, he said loudly, "Who is it?"

"Eve."

"What do you want?"

"Some advice, mind if I come in? I need to talk for a moment."

Recognising her voice, Seethan opened the door. As he did so, he popped his head out and searched both sides of the darkened corridor as she entered, but there was nothing there. He shut the door and turned to face Eve. Standing several paces away the wind breezed through the half-open window and ruffled her white-cotton nightdress. The half-moon shone through the garment easily outlining her figure. He swallowed.

"What is it, how can I help?"

"First question, if you had offspring would they be babies or puppies?"

At the look on his face she added, "Sorry, I'm trying to lighten the mood. You look a bit uptight."

"Do you blame me?"

"Not really. I brought wine," she lifted the bottle. "Shall we share a glass?"

He sighed. "What is it you want, Eve?"

She bit her lip, opened the green bottle and poured some of the deep-red contents into the single glass next to his bed. Then she sat on the sheet-covered straw mattress and sipped from the bottle, raising it in a toast as she said simply, "Cheers."

Seethan took the glass and raised it to clink against the bottle.

"What's wrong with me, Seethan?"

"Nothing. Well…we all have a few screws loose."

"Don't fool around, you know what I mean. I'm in love with you, and I can't help it. Your Rose is gone, she's no longer exists. I'd say she's dead but she was never alive in the first place, as I understand it. I'm here and I can offer so much. This is absolute hell for me. Why won't you at least let me try?"

"Because I still love her."

Eve scowled. "That didn't stop you making puppy eyes at that female werewolf." At the look of shock and hurt in his eyes, she took a deep breath and apologised." I'm sorry Seethan, that was unfair. But if you think about it Rose wasn't even human. I can warm your bed. You can feel my heart through my chest, feel the pulse in my veins. Look at me, Seethan. I'm alive! Who knows what tomorrow will bring? Please, all I'm asking is for you to just to give me a chance. Even if it's for this one night."

Seethan realised then that he was only wearing his shorts. It hadn't been intentional. He'd responded to the tap on his door of instinct, and hadn't taken the time to put anything else on, only to grasp the knife that might be needed to save his life. Eve hadn't looked at his body though, only into his eyes. Hers now glistened with tears.

"Eve, I…"

"You saved my brother's life! He and I have yet to find a way to help you, but this is apart from that."

"You owe me nothing. Rose was my life. She was the only person I have ever cared for. Sure, I loved Mrs M who practically adopted me, and of course my parents – what I can remember of them. But with her it was different. I'm still not over her loss, and to be honest I doubt I will be."

Eve reached up and put her hand on his shoulder. Eyes almost begging, a single tear trickled down her left cheek. "You don't have to make love to me, Seethan. Just hold me. Let me stay with you tonight so... so that I don't have to be alone."

For an answer, Seethan led the way to the bed. He turned back the quilt and sheet on her side and then climbed into the other. Eve shrugged off her slip and slid in beside him. Her arms snaked around him, pulling herself closer. Her breasts flattened against his chest, Seethan fought the urge within him, to stop his arousal but it was no use. Biting down his desire he rolled over, pushing his back into her. He could sense her disappointment, but he just couldn't betray Rose again.

"Go to sleep," he said after a while. "We have a long day tomorrow."

Eve didn't say anything. Not a word. But Seethan was comforted by the sound of her breathing and the warmth of her arms around him, her body close to his. Her breathing gradually quietened into a gentle rhythmic shushing, like waves on a beach. His desire was still strong but he fought it, ignoring her hands looping over to his chest and the warm naked skin on his back.

Before he knew it, he too was asleep.

*****

Seethan was woken from nightmares a couple of times by Eve shaking him, before drifting off again. But when he finally awoke on his own, it was to a bone-deep chill. He felt frozen, unable to move. A clammy feeling clawed up his back and into his shoulders, his muscles went rigid. He wanted to scream but was unable to do so, no matter how hard he tried, all that came out was a low moan. There was a strangled gasp from Eve beside him. Her fingers dug into his skin, her nails ripping and clawing. He knew what it was, having been here before. But poor Eve had no clue what-so-ever, only that utter dread that reached deep into your soul.

The outline of a man stood in the darkness opposite him, making that remote corner of the room even murkier. There was no sound, just that terrifying sense of foreboding. Again Seethan tried to speak but couldn't, nor could he move or drag his eyes away and wish the apparition was gone. Both their eyes were drawn to the thing that stood there.

The figure took a pace forward and Seethan drew in his breath with a hiss. It was Pete Philips, the brother of his best friend Steff. Pete had died long ago, in the crash that had killed the rest of the team and left Seethan with PTSD. Pete's head was badly battered and blood trickled down the shreds of his neck and over his green flight suit. It dripped from his left breast pocket onto the floor, with a light *tap tap tap*.

Pete's left arm bore the black commando badge of special forces. His left arm bore the emblem of their squadron, a howling wolf – which was ironic given Seethan's lycanthropy. Dead eyes gazed sightlessly from a gaunt head that sat above that thin, bedraggled throat. Seethan knew that this wasn't Pete, for he'd seen the man's head completely destroyed, but here he was. In his mind he could see that shattered corpse in the cockpit, an echo of what was here in front of him now.

"Pete…" Seethan gasped. "Why are you here?"

"I came to warn you," came a low rasping voice from everywhere. It was like a whisper, only quieter, yet oddly clear. "You have to stop the Dark Ones, before it's too late. This is only the beginning, unless you resolve this there's far worse to come."

"Too late for what?" Seethan managed to croak. He heard a squeak from behind him and – even with his back to her – he sensed that Eve had managed to sit up in bed, staring in horror at the apparition before them. Her terrified eyes were agog, her mouth half open as if in mid-scream.

The ghostly Pete crept forward, until he was just inches from the bed. Blood from his battered body landed with wet splashes on the floor. It was him, all right.

"You need to stop them," Pete repeated, in a voice that sounded like leaves whispering in the wind.

"We're here to try and we'll do our best, I promise you that. Look, Pete…is…is Rose there with you?"

"No." The answer was a firm dry rustle.

"She must be!" Seethan cried defiantly. "Just because she was an android doesn't mean she didn't have a soul. I know for a fact that she did, Rose has to be there with you, somewhere."

It was weird asking a question of a corpse, and yet Seethan found himself talking to it as if all this were normal.

"She loved me and I her. You need a soul to experience that."

"She also might have just said anything to please you. After all, that's what they're designed for." Pete hissed.

"Fuck you, Pete! I *know* she had a soul. She must be there somewhere. Please, can you look?"

"That's all that matters to you, isn't it."

And then, suddenly, Pete was gone.

Seethan jerked awake suddenly. He was still curled up, with Eve next to him. Had he dreamt all of this? He turned over and sat up to face her.

"Eve, are you okay?"

She too was awake now, her eyes filled with terror. She sat up and clung to him fiercely. "Is that what you go through, every time, with the dead?"

"Basically, although sometimes they just want to talk. I'm lucky that they can contact me. I don't begrudge them it at all."

She jerked away from him breasts hanging loose. A single strand of almost black hair had fallen over one of those brown eyes. She brushed it aside almost angrily. "Seethan, are you insane? They are dead, that's *D E A D*. There's nothing normal about talking to ghosts."

"Pete may be dead but he still came to warn me," Seethan murmured. "It's not just me, because you saw him too."

Eve scrambled from the bed and ran naked to the door. "Fuck you, Seethan Bodell. If that's what being with you means I have to go through, then forget what I've said."

As the door slammed shut, Seethan lay back, a slight smile on his face. She may be gone now but the image of her pert backside disappearing out of the door remained stamped in his mind. Maybe she'd leave him alone now, but he doubted it. She was just scared, and who could blame her? He knew that she'd seen the dead once before, during that last battle, when they came to help against the colonial army. He didn't blame her. After all, who'd willingly want to consort with the dead?

Why had it never been Rose who came back? He had betrayed her before, with Fae, and he'd never forgiven himself. While in wolf form and unable to control himself, he'd taken Fae off Andy and became pack leader, only to abandon her later when he finally came to his senses and realised what he'd done. Andy had taken over the pack once again, and Seethan had let him do so without complaint. Andy had displayed his dominance by rutting with Fae right in front of him, her eyes staring into his while it happened. Although Fae preferred Seethan, it was as much about her cementing her role within the pack as lead female as it was about Andy claiming his own dominance. Many times, as a wolf, Seethan had the urge to tear them apart. It was no longer his place; that was with Rose and he knew it. But how long could he hang on to a love that's no longer there?

It was fairly early and still dark outside, but Seethan washed in a basin of cold water and then shrugged on his clothes. Habitually early risers the others were already downstairs ahead of him, eating hot buttered toast spread liberally with jam or honey. Seeing him enter, Eve turned away from him, trying to hide the hurt in her eyes. The odd thing was, she understood him and his feelings. She wished someone could love her as much as Seethan did Rose. The others glanced from one to the other, looking confused. It was as if they could tell that something had happened, but not what.

"Erm…did we miss something?" Shipman finally said.

"Yes," Seethan replied. "I had a visitor last night. My friend Pete came to see me."

"And, I take it there's more to this?" Shipman said, raising his eyebrows.

"Well, for starters he's been dead four years – even longer by your reckoning. Weird, I know, but there you go."

"And this ghost, what did he want?" Shipman persisted.

"He said that we have to stop the Dark Ones, whoever they are. I think that there's more going on than we know. We need to get our fingers out and get a move on."

"So, what's the plan?" Eve asked.

"As much as I hate to say it," Seethan admitted. "I think our only option is to go and see Tiandra, the fairy queen."

"First," Shona interjected. "To do that we need to find Willow. While banished from the fairy kingdom she won't have gone far, and I think I know where she'll be.'

Chapter 10

"So, where are we?" Seethan asked several days later, as they stopped to rest for a moment.

"We're at the edge of the Seelie realm," Shona replied. "I've heard that the Unseelie are contesting parts of it, through third parties of course."

The darkness, as night fell, brought a series of distant coughing roars. All eyes turned to Olaf but he just looked back at them in surprise.

"Sounds like a tyger," Andrews said.

"It does," Eve agreed. "Bound to be some about but let's just hope it stays the hell away from us, we have enough trouble as it is. I have to say that I've heard it now and again before – or others like it – but it always sounded far away, enough to not be a problem. Hopefully, it'll stay that way."

Conversation faltered for a moment, and then Seethan said to Shona, "Has Willow been hiding here all this time?"

"No. When she was banished, she went and stayed with the elves for a while, seeking sanctuary until she was sure it was safe to come here. Willow likes being close to home, even though she cannot actually return until the banishment is lifted – if it ever is."

"How will we find her?" Commodore Andrews said.

"We won't need to, she'll find us."

As twilight fell Shona's words proved prophetic. It started with a red firefly-like light flittering amidst the trees. It hovered on the edges of their camp for a while, until the witch stood up and beckoned to it. The glimmer approached and Seethan saw it was a tiny human with filmy wings. And then, with a flash of light, Willow stood before them human-sized. She had long dark hair with startling deep-red slashes running down through it at the front. Her eyes were a light sky-blue, lips a bright red – matching the streaks in her hair. Her wings were also crimson, the interspaces of which had thin black edging that made them look like linked cells. The wings themselves hung from the level of her shoulders, reaching up to her head and then swooping down to the base of her back – where their unity was broken by several long black cilia, each as thick as a man's thumb.

Seethan was startled. The woman was comely and kind-looking. The top half of her dress a semi-transparent red bodice, through which her areola could be glimpsed, the rear of her outfit was black and sheer. Those skirts were as red as blood and hung down past her knees, the long tapering legs themselves leading to crimson shoes.

"Hello, Willow. I'm Shona."

"I know who you are; the elves said you would come. They also told me the terrible thing the ants did to the village, even though they couldn't control it. It's awful, not only for those that suffered but also for the creatures that did it, they have the burden to contend with. Thankfully I managed to get a message to the queen about it and she succeeded in nullifying the spell over them – now your friend there." She pointed.

"I'm…Chovy. Thanks for your part in releasing me. I'm forever in your debt."

"Not a problem. After all, it was our brethren that caused it. The fairy folk were never like this before, so whatever's going on needs to stop. As for you, Seethan Bodell, the elves remember and said to inform you that they still owe you their allegiance."

Andrews explained why they were there, to stop the Fey using changelings to replace people in the colonies, and to try and find out why they were doing it.

As he spoke, Willow looked puzzled at first. The wind caused wisps of her hair to flit back and forth across her forehead and those inquisitive blue eyes. She brushed it aside and said softly, "That may have happened in times long past but now the use of changelings is strictly forbidden. That's what caused mankind to become aware of us in the first place, and no-doubt the resulting trouble between us. Eventually, as magic retreated from this world, we fled en-masse to the hidden lands as did so many other races. But, if what you say is true, then this suggests something very strange is going on."

"Well, there's a good reason to join forces with us," Seethan said. "We all want to stop this. Will you come with us?"

"Yes, and I'll get another message to the queen. As you know, I can't return to the realm unless invited. I'm just hoping she'll agree to a meeting."

"Sounds like a plan to me," Seethan said, joining in. "Looks like we have a way ahead."

*****

Early next morning a bumblebee appeared and, with a loud but dull buzzing, lazily approached Willow. The bee was a queen, and Willow told them that it said that most of her hive had already died due to the yearly drop in temperature. She herself should have been finding somewhere secure to slumber – to awaken when things warmed once again – but had caught Willow's cry for help and come to see what she could do.

The bee buzzed about Willow for a while and then, like a heavy transporter, droned back the way she had come. A while later, she returned.

"Good news," Willow said. "As you are here, Queen Tiandra has agreed to meet with us but it will mean summoning all of our kind, including the Unseelie. This is because every one of us has a say in what we do, although the final decision remains with Tiandra. It will be dangerous – be sure that this is what you want."

"It's what we're here for, right?" Seethan said. "As they say in my time, take us to your leader."

With a half-smile Willow waved her wand. Instantly there was a snap and she changed back into that tiny glowing red figure. Fluttering, she led the way into the forest.

*****

139

Andrews looked confused, as they reached the base of a huge grassy mound. At the very top stood a single oak tree, much like a silent guardian. It had a thick tawny trunk, up which were dark finger-deep cracks as if running towards the far branches and those few remaining leaves that were a mixture of copper, deep-reds, and burnished-gold.

"What is this place?" Andrews asked.

"This is one of our most sacred Dun Forts. Within is the path to the Golden Shores, those distant lands to which we retreat in times of crisis. It's not common knowledge. The entrance is well hidden and no one will find it unless they know the way."

Initially Seethan felt that Willow was going to lead them within the fort but instead they continued into the forest a short distance until they reached a dark but moonlit grassy knoll, surrounded on several sides by immense mushrooms of various types. Some of these were white, others orange. A few arose like layered cakes of yellow, jutting widely like platforms and upon them sat a few small figures. Many had a pale strawberry top – bright red with white spots which were visible even in the limited light and much like those in the books Seethan had read as a child. More than a few stood like imposing sentinels – tall, thin, and grey – their visage somehow stern, aloof, and threatening. They surrounded a circle of cropped grass, on which stood high-backed stone chairs. Each looked carefully crafted, with forest scenes that were worn down with age. Above each chair floated a small orb of light, just bright enough to illuminate them.

"What is *this* place?" Seethan asked, as they stepped onto the dirt pathway that ringed the place. The path was covered with a carpet of rotting vegetation, which crumbled and crunched underfoot like brittle bone. When he spoke again his voice echoed in the darkness. "Doesn't the Queen live in a palace?"

"She did, of a kind, but when the Fey people split our home fell. You see, it was the symbolism of our union, our beating heart so's to speak. My father built it when we returned to this world. He'd be broken – like the tower or castle – to learn of it. So, for now, this is our meeting place and where all of us come to make important decisions." Willow answered. "Each of us can speak, but Tiandra is still our queen."

She ushered each of them to the seats. Chovy's soon ran black with thousands of ants, as he spread himself over and around it.

"Is it me," Seethan said quizzically, "or are there more of you ants now."

"Yes, many have joined our nest. This is a first for Antkind – until now we have only protected our own nests and never joined with another. But now our hives have spoken and they understand our pain and the danger. Many have sent their warriors to do battle against the evil ones."

Seethan didn't know what to say. Instead, he turned to watch a throng of fairy folk slip through the mushrooms and stand silently around the perimeter. They were all manner of shape and sizes, with a few sitting atop beetles no larger than they themselves. Others climbed aboard the mushrooms, or regarded them from a variety of beetles taller than Seethan himself. A warning trumpet sounded and everyone rose to their feet, as a voice announced, "Please welcome Tiandra, Queen of the Fey."

The fairy queen approached. Standing just below Seethan's chin her brown eyes and kindly face bore a sense of warmth that was in sharp contrast with her snow-white skin. Her frost-white wings were spread widely, those skirts a light-Lincoln-green interspaced with downward slashes of brown – both of which bore symbols that Seethan didn't recognise. That shoulder-length hair was light brown and the white bodice thinly bordered by struts of the same green. She spread her skirts as she sat on a seat much larger than the others.

"Willow," Tiandra said, her voice ringing as clear as a bell. "You have been granted passage here today to discuss an issue that you say is a threat to our people. Speak!" The last word, definitely a command, rang like a gong through the assembly.

Willow's chin rose in determination, as she stood up from her chair. "I've come here to tell you that parties, other than those allowed, have been using the gateways, and have gained access to the colony worlds. Human children living there are being snatched from their families and replaced by changelings, or just killed."

"What?" Tiandra gasped; her eyes wide with shock. "That's impossible, no changeling has been authorised for generations. It was part of our pact with the Spooks for our return to this world. We agreed that we would not use changelings against the humans as we once did – and we have kept our word!"

"None-the-less, your Majesty, what I say is true. And there have been other goings on too. Plagues of animals and insects have beset the human villages, as you have become aware. One such event is a rarity, but these were many and I happen to know for a fact that these were caused by the Unseelie."

"Oh my!" screeched a woman clad from head to foot in shiny black armour and riding a huge spider. She led a long line of others, clad similarly, emerging from the darkness. Within it, Seethan could make out the swirling mist of a portal.

The woman was a mirror image of the queen, even down to the shoulder-length hair. It was the cruel expression she wore that differed between them. Around Mabe stood Fey warriors. Originally the army had been one but torn by loyalty had now split, so some stood with Tiandra and others with Mabe – all clad in their multi-coloured seashell armour, clasping spears, atop pinkish pigs. Amidst those behind Mabe these were interspaced with shortish black-cowled figures, a bit like miniature monks. Others rode skinny green-coloured praying mantises that stretched upwards and were taller than Seethan himself. There were beetles, pigs, and other spiders. These long rows vanished into the darkness behind Mabe.

Seethan shuddered. *God*, he thought – *spiders*! Particularly anything that was his own chest height, evil-looking, and covered in coarse bristly hair.

Her mount was incredibly dark and, with her outfit, she seemed to blend into it so they became one. The segmented legs of the creature gleamed like polished black rock and those huge scythe-like jaws hung close to the ground.

"That's Mabe, the queen's sister," Shona whispered to the others. She couldn't say more because the other screeched over her.

"Willow," Mabe declared, "Years back you had the audacity to set my sister and I against each other. Now you dare to lie about me in front of her?"

"It's no lie," Commodore Andrews said, interrupting loudly as he stepped forward a pace. "It's actually why Lieutenant Shipman and I came here in the first place, to try and stop whatever's going on and to find a way forward – to prevent another war between our races."

Willow spoke again, her voice carrying clearly against the sudden silence. "And how is it that you can sit on that spider, my lady? Those creatures catch and kill many of us every year, all Fey despise them. Why are you so suddenly different from the rest of us?"

"Oh, well you see, this little beauty is easily controlled with a little magic. Why waste such resources?" Mabe simpered, again combing her hair aside with long thin white fingers tipped with black pointed fingernails.

Shona again spoke quietly to Seethan and the others. "Looks like those behind Mabe are *her* followers alone, nothing to do with the Seelie now."

"That's one hell of a lot of bad guys," Seethan said. His tone changed slightly. "Commodore, didn't you say you were a policeman before being recalled to the service? If so, can't you go and arrest that God-awful fucking thing she's riding?"

"He wouldn't have enough handcuffs," Shipman said drily.

"Actually, that's quite funny," Seethan replied with a smirk, while trying unsuccessfully to swallow.

"Mabe," the queen said. "When our father died he left me to rule as sole monarch and I know that you took this badly. However, it was his decision to make not mine. I'm simply following his orders and fulfilling his wishes, as should you. Explain to me exactly what's going on here?"

Mabe chuckled drily. "You may or may not know that a race known as The Dark Ones have plundered this world for centuries. They hunted mankind unimpeded and unseen, and the humans didn't even question why so many of their number were disappearing. Before the Sundering they were losing almost a quarter of a million people a year but they just shrugged it off. But after most of mankind had either been killed or had left this world for their colonies, those predators still needed feeding. With so few humans what do you think happened? They began taking the Fey instead. One day they captured me, a Princess and your sister, and you didn't even care that I'd gone missing."

"Not true. I was unaware of it," Tiandra said, "but you were always running off to one place or another. You'd be gone for days, sometimes weeks."

"Be that as it may, when I needed you, you weren't there. So, the Dark Ones took me and I had to make a bargain."

"How so?" Tiandra growled.

Mabe continued. "They said they would not prey on the Fey anymore if, in return, we allowed them usage of the gateways to the human colonies. It was an easy choice. As far as I was concerned, they could do what they wished with the humans. There was a slight problem, however. Only one, or two at most, can travel those paths at a time without alerting the Spooks, and no technology can be carried through it. It's a bit like the Spooks' null field around Earth stopping human technology from working."

"Why do I know nothing of this?"

"Because, dear sister, I didn't tell you," Mabe replied. "Let's face it, I knew you'd be angry. But despite what you may think, I complied with your exact orders. Your words to me long ago were, '*I was to take no human, or other creature on this world, and replace them with changelings'*. Well, I didn't. I simply opened the gateways that led to the colonies and let the Dark Ones take their prey from there. After all, I'd much rather it was them than us. Don't you agree?"

"Just who, or what, are these *Dark Ones*?"

Mabe was silent for a moment but then finally spoke. "They are the Shades of Darkness, creatures from beyond the far realms. They too have ships that can travel between the stars but they don't want to use them in case they're spotted by human instruments. Instead, they now have the gateways."

"And you enabled this?" Tiandra's voice was filled with fury. "After they fed on our own people, you allowed them to feast on humans? What were you thinking? The Spooks will relegate us to the twilight lands once again!"

"The Humans are a blight!" Mabe snapped. "They should be exterminated. The Dark Ones have promised to do this and, in return, they will leave us here on Earth in peace."

"And you actually believe that?" Tiandra said. "If so, you are far more a fool than I thought."

"Why are they doing this?" Commodore Andrews asked. "We could supply them with so many alternatives. Why haven't they spoken to us directly?"

Mabe snorted. "Would you discuss options with a cow or a chicken? Human children are easier to catch and replace than their adults. They barely notice or even question them, and practically ignore them most of the times. Our changelings gather intelligence on your military bases and feed it back to The Dark Ones, while they themselves gather their fleet. Although they covert your colonies, we Fey are content with this one world. We are not a threat to them." Spit flecked Mabe's lips as she spoke.

"Listen, we can still negotiate and that's why I'm here." Andrews insisted. "Meat consumption is banned on most of our worlds and so we've developed many alternatives, these would easily allow us to co-exist peacefully."

"What, as peacefully as you did with the Spooks?" Mabe's eyes glittered. "You attacked them the instant you knew they existed! How long before you plotted against the Shades and then attacked them when you were finally ready?"

"The Spooks attacked us first! We didn't even know they were there when we landed on Halloween, they hid themselves well. It was only when they began slaughtering our people that we finally retaliated. But that's old news and long past. There is no conflict between our peoples now."

Mabe laughed. "Whatever. The Dark Ones are coming for you Commodore, and they're hungry…"

There was a long silence, which was again broken by Mabe. "Are you with me, sister, or do you stand against me?"

"With you? What you've done is evil! We'll end up paying the price, I'm sure. I cannot condone this, I will not! We stand against you and will block all that you do!"

"Then it's just as well I brought allies, isn't it?"

Tiandra held up one hand, palm out, and said loudly, "Fey do not attack Fey." Then she paused and one eyebrow arched. "Willow raised an interesting question just now. How is it you ride a spider? My sister would never do that, she hated and feared them so. Who are you? Because you are certainly not Mabe."

"Don't you see?" Andrews interjected. "She's a changeling! Your sister's gone; they've already replaced her."

As he spoke a golden sunrise rose from behind the lines of Dark Ones, illuminating all in a burnished-bronze glow. It glinted from the tips of thousands of spears, but cast the hooded shapes into even darker silhouettes.

"Ah, I see our little plot has been revealed," Mabe said, her lips curling into a cruel smile. "Your sister was captured before we made this deal. Although she designed and brokered it, that meant she wasn't bound by its constraints, for she was already a prisoner. Consequently, she was invited to dinner and replaced by myself – a simulacrum if you will. But in the process part of the original person remains, like a shadow cast by firelight onto the wall of a cave. Your sister is within me. I can see her shape even now flickering on the parapets of my mind; hear her voice begging for release."

Mabe's cackling laugh echoed through the clearing. Suddenly she bit off a command in a guttural tongue and many of her followers atop their varied and horrific mounts instantly launched the spears they were carrying at the multitude of Fey clustered around the circle of seats.

It was as if a wave had slammed into the defenceless Fey. They fell by the hundreds, whilst other spears clattered off their seashell armour. Tiandra's surviving warriors lowered their spears in shock and looked aghast, as if unbelieving and unsure what to do. The queen's words echoed in Seethan's ears, *Fey do not attack Fey!* They hadn't expected this; they thought their kin wouldn't hurt them. It was then that he realised why they stood with Mabe.

"They aren't your kin; they're Changelings!" Seethan shouted. Knowing that, one by one, they must have all been taken and replaced. "Fight, you aren't breaking any vows, they are all Shades!"

He darted in front of Tiandra, smashing aside spears as they were flung towards her. With a horrid thump one of them slammed into his shoulder spinning him around and dropping him to his knees. He rose and tore it free, knocking another incoming projectile aside with a forearm. His face filled with pain and rage, as he bellowed, "Olaf, now!"

Even as he spoke Seethan transformed. There was no time to discard his clothes, he simply tore them to shreds. The werewolf within him howled and leapt towards the enemy. To one side he heard an answering roar, and a large muscular tawny shape shot past him. Seethan instantly recognised the tyger that Olaf had become. Answering howls came from the darkness around them; his pack had finally arrived, just as he'd asked. The multitude of wolves tore into the enemy, creating chaos in the storm-tossed melee as the Fey began to fight back.

Together the were-creatures cut into the enemy, but before they got there Tiandra began to chant. Her voice was light and musical, yet its melody cut through the din of battle like a knife.

As she sang yet another sound arose, one Seethan had heard before. It was like a foghorn, the forlorn cry of a lonely ship on a fog-laden sea. He felt a surge of hope then, as a chill wind rose over the constant gentle one. Some of the Dark Ones stopped and milled about in confusion, while others of their kin fought on.

It was Hell's Orchestra, the nightmare melody of dull horns and out-of-tune trumpeting. His ears, more sensitive than most, ached as a rising wave of drumbeats thundered in the early morning. The Wild Hunt burst into view, tearing like a tsunami through the towering mushrooms, many of which were shattered by the assault. Waves of silver-clad elven warriors thundered towards the foe, armour gleaming in the sunlight. Hundreds of the enemy ripped off their helmets and tore at their ears as the Wild Hunt smashed into them and flung them aside as if they were mere kindling. The elves rode all manner of beast; horses, bears, giant cats, and wolves. Each of the mounts vocalised their displeasure, adding to the furore.

Still Tiandra sang, the soft lilt of her voice rising to cut through the din. Suddenly, the Unseelie mounts staggered as if hit by a great force. They reared back; hooves, claws, and paws scrambling frantically at the air. And then they rebelled and turned on their riders, as the Seelie Queen broke the spell that bound them. Chovy dissolved into a carpet of ants that flowed towards and over their foe. The gigantic spider that Mabe had been riding raised its front legs as if it were praying. The sudden motion threw Mabe backwards and off her mount and she fell with a screech that was cut short as she impacted the ground.

Stunned and trying feebly to sit up, Mabe shuffled away from the arachnid. But the creature was intent on her. It's needle-like teeth stabbed downwards and into her chest, and then the forelegs snatched at her and held her tight as the venom pumped into her, melting her insides. Seethan couldn't take his eyes off her as the spider held her tight as if in a macabre hug. He watched as her screams intensified, her face and body bloating. And then it was as if she were melting, and the spider begun sucking up the soup from inside her.

Not one of the Unseelie mounts attacked Tiandra's supporters. It was as if they knew who had enslaved them, and were keen on their revenge. The bottle-green, three-segmented praying mantises had four limbs on their rear sections with two much thicker and longer ones closer to their heads. These top arms were equipped with vicious-looking barbs, which they used to hold their victims in place as they snatched them up. Holding their prey tightly, the triangular heads swivelled as if in question, causing their antennae to whip back and forth. Large bulbous green eyes with small black centres were stuck on each side of their heads as if in an afterthought. The jaws on triangular heads swivelled once again, as they reached down and tore into their former riders.

The Dark armies marched through the churning portal, not caring any longer about alerting the Spooks for that time was well past. There were thousands of the dark robed Shades and their Fey kin. But armed as they were with spears and long-bladed knives, they stood no chance against the onslaught of mantises, spiders, ants and were-creatures that turned and crashed like a tidal wave against them.

Wolf Seethan sprang through the legs of one of the huge insects as it held a Shade aloft and those massive jaws chewed away at its face. The cloaked creature ceased screaming non-sensible words in a high-pitched voice, as its features disappeared in chunks down the insect's throat. Seethan closed his jaws around the hooded face of a Shade, biting deeply and shaking it from side to side. He felt the crunch of bone between his jaws as his teeth met in the middle, and then he spat out the bloodied mush that remained.

Olaf smashed the enemy aside with claws like swords and teeth like daggers. He stood forepaws on the fallen, tearing off chunks of their bodies and throwing the remains aside. His roars echoed through the mushroom forest, and suddenly, it was met by an answering roar as a second tyger joined the fray. Seethan knew who it was, even without looking; he'd been waiting for her to act.

It was Molly. Like Olaf, the barmaid had also been injured by the were-tyger and had suffered Olaf's fate. Seethan had sensed her following them at a distance but had said nothing about it to the others. At times he'd gone in secret to teach her to control her change and, to his surprise, she'd picked it up quite quickly – much more so than he himself had at first.

Molly swept through the enemy like a tornado, batting the Dark Ones aside as if they were kindling. With her jaws clasped around the middle of a shrieking Shade her paws slashed at two others, before she bit the one in her mouth into two. The Dark One's blood was an odd brown colour, and it splattered like a muddy rainfall.

Seethan knew that he had to seal the gateway in the darkness from which the Shades were coming but he didn't know how. And then, all of a sudden, he had it.

"Nadons, are you there?" Seethan growled. "If so, we could do with a hand!" But there was no reply. Nothing. Only the sound of battle; weapons against shield, teeth against flesh, and constant screams of the injured and dying.

He'd hoped that Nadons, the Spook he'd had dealings with in the past, had been monitoring them – that he might hear, and come to their rescue. He had done so in the past, but Seethan feared it was a forlorn hope.

After the Spook War, and the aliens had finally climbed out of their fog of insanity they had, in a way, begun to care for those few human survivors – as if ashamed at what they had done. Even now, the Spooks went a little mad occasionally. It was as if they were still twisted with grief at the loss of their kin and homeworld. Seethan could understand that. It was a constant mix of grief, terror, love, and joy. One moment they were helping the humans with their various gifts of magic, the next something wicked knocked on your door. It was a world of insanity, as if they knew they were mad but strove unsuccessfully to overcome it. If only he could reach them.

A bone-chilling groan came from the darkness. It was as if a long unused and rusty door were slowly creaking open. The Shades and their followers faltered, looking around them. And then they froze in fear. Seethan heard Andrews and Shipman catch their breaths, as they saw the dim faltering shapes emerging from the darkness. With it came a stench that he recognised well, always made him want to retch. The dead have a disgusting odour that you never got used to and which you wanted to forever block from your mind. It was the reek of rotting flesh, it took your breath away and made you want to vomit. Once again, the dead had heard Seethan's call for help and they had answered. In his mind he could see the dead pushing aside the clods of earth above them. Dragging themselves from their graves they fought their ways out of sepulchres, pushing aside grave covers and toppling tombstones. Even ancient seelie warriors answered the call, their forms adding to the army. The dead were coming, travelling through the gateways, and even though he knew they were on his side Seethan felt a deep sense of unease, even dread.

The Shade's spears and swords slashed and stabbed at the corpses but it did no good. Although the cadavers fell in their hundreds, unable to continue on, others filled their place, for the dead were beyond numerous. The fallen crawled on, leaving trails of putrid discarded flesh in their wake. Those lifeless bodies didn't have much strength but they could trip, bite, and tear. Many had been buried with weaponry, and those that weren't quickly scavenged fallen blades from the battlefield; all joined in the slaughter of the Shade army.

Their main power, though, lay in fear. For when one of the dead gazed at you, the hollow of their eyes reached deep into your soul and seemed to find you wanting.

More of the elven cavalry smashed into the enemy, the dead flinging them aside while the wolves and tygers bit and clawed at them unremittingly. And then they broke. One by one the Shades turned and cleared the field, with some falling even as they tried – overcome by the armies of ants that flowed over them devouring all as they went.

Shona raised both hands and a large ball of bright blue energy flashed into being, casting off iridescent sparks of unbelievable power. She hurled the eye-searing orb at the now wholly retreating horde, watching as it burned a clear path through their numbers. She turned her face upwards and bellowed, her eyes a bright cobalt as intermittent blue beams of energy slashed like a scythe through the enemy ranks.

And then, just like that, the Shades were gone. Back through the gateway to whatever hell it was that had spawned them. But before that gateway closed their former mounts followed, constantly chomping at their flanks. Some of the larger creatures picking them up and throwing them aside in a spray of blood; a galloping cascade of unbelievable horror until at last the gateway blinked out, locking their rides alongside them in whatever hell-hole they'd crawled from. Here and there a few of the Shades fought on unable to reach safety, trapped in gradually reducing piles of insects.

As silence fell Seethan changed back into human form and stood there for some time naked, his breath clouding white on the frigid air, while cries from the injured and dying rang like trumpets through the sudden stillness. A few of the spiders and mantises remained once the gateway had closed, but once it did so they reverted to their normal size. They turned and fled as one, rather than stay and face the ire of the Fey.

And then it was all over.

Chapter 11

Seethan bitterly surveyed the battlefield, the thousands of dead. Even the previously deceased had fallen again. Watching as the elves finished off the dying, taking away the enemy heads and weapons as bizarre war trophies. He saw something then that he hadn't before, the constantly cowled faces of the enemy were unveiled to reveal scaly, golden, reptilian heads – much more like slender lizards than frogs although they too had wide lipless mouths. Their eyes were shaped like a human's, but their corneas were like battered bronze speckled with gold which expanded to the iris surrounding a pitch-black pupil that now gazed into nothingness.

The gateway had closed, the first time Seethan had seen this happen and he wondered whether this had sealed forever, or would perhaps open at a later date. It was something he'd have to investigate somehow. Soon the elves had turned and left without a word, which left only the Fey, Seethan and his friends and the countless corpses. Even the pack had left; with Seethan, Olaf, and Molly transitioning back to naked humans. A carpet of ants marched towards one spot, where their growing mound gradually coalesced back into Chovy, swollen overtime by additional ant armies.

The Fey held expressions like children who'd been caught misbehaving, horrified at what they'd done. They withdrew from the carnage and clustered in groups, squatting on their knees and clutching each other. Many ignored their own issues and sought to help injured friends and comrades, while tears ran down blood-streaked faces. Seethan had the distinct feeling that they were unused to battle, unlike the harsher snow-faced elves whose countenances had remained stern and unyielding as their shimmering silver lances and swords had finished off the enemy that lay shrieking on the ground. Only a few of the fairy remained of those in the shell armour they'd donned in apparent tradition – or perhaps out of desperation.

Still naked, Molly turned to face an incredulous Commodore Andrews. "I'm sorry, I didn't realise what was happening to me at first; and when I did I didn't know how to tell you. It was such a small wound, how was I to know? And then..." Her voice trailed off, as Andrews shook his head, as if unsure what to say.

Seethan turned away to let them sort it out with as much privacy as possible. For as much as he'd have like to see them staying together, he couldn't see it happening. Shipman and the commodore would return to the colonies and he just couldn't see Molly joining him there. She was stuck on this world now and, in any case, there would be no place for her out there.

A figure wove through the crowd and Seethan found himself facing an old, white-bearded man of a similar size to him, wearing a worn-looking dun-coloured cape; the hood of which was thrown back to reveal eyes that gleamed like windows into the darkness of space. He repressed a shudder. Nadons had finally answered his call.

"Thanks for coming, although we could have used your help a little earlier," Seethan said, as Shipman tossed him that old pair of shorts with a look that said, *return those buggers washed, this time!*

"Oh, we were here but this wasn't really our battle," Nadons said. He coughed and leant on a heavily-carved and weathered-looking, dark-wooden walking staff. "You humans must look out for yourselves."

"We know that. But if only we could have negotiated a peace treaty with these Dark Ones that would have been the best victory here. Now, it seems, we could end up at war with them."

Andrews and Shipman joined them, as Nadons said, "Could? You already are, you just haven't realised it yet."

"They'll come then?" Andrews asked.

"Yes, eventually, and when they do you'd better be ready."

"There must be something we can do to prevent this?" Andrews insisted. He pulled a small silver flask from a pocket and took a quick pull, swallowed and savoured the taste. His eyes held a rheumy and desperate look.

"Trust me we have tried to help, ourselves," Nadons said. "In return for peace we even offered to let them use the gateways for small parties of their people to travel back and forth between worlds, apart from those belonging to humans of course – or for any military reason. They disagreed, seemingly intent on your destruction. This leaves us with no option but to put guardians in the gateways."

"Might be a good idea, but will it stop the Dark Ones?"

Nadons tilted his head and shrugged, as he rubbed a white-moustached nose with a somewhat grubby hand. "From using the gateways, or for coming for you? You already know they they have ships, much as you do, and they are gradually building up their fleet. Sooner or later they *will* come, so you have to prepare."

"What if they want the Earth, as well as the colonies?" Seethan persisted. "And from their actions here today it looks like they do."

"If they try we will fight to protect it."

"In which case we will be on the same side for once. If it comes down to defending Earth, humanity will stand beside you."

Nadons' harrumphed. "We'll do what we must. But, in the meantime, I'd get going if I were you. Now the Shadows know you're aware of them you can expect an attack at any time. And who knows what they've already learned of your capabilities and military power? Some of them are no doubt deeply embedded in your military – perhaps even your command structure. Were I human, I'd be pretty worried right now."

"We better leave now then. I take it that we have your permission? We have a war to prepare for; in what little time is left, that is."

"Yes, you can leave this world," Nadons replied. "Although I suspect that you and I will meet again in the not-too-distant future. I just pray that it's for better reasons than the last time we did so."

"Indeed," Andrews said, and summoned the others.

*****

Seethan, Shipman, and Andrews were standing before the sealed door to their landing craft. The others were standing to one side, watching them.

Seethan still couldn't quite believe that the Spooks were actually allowing the two men to leave Earth. Perhaps this was a good omen for future relations. It certainly went to show how much the Spooks had changed. He found himself nodding towards Shipman as the man entered the craft, leaving the hatch open. Seethan stretched his hand towards the commodore, who shook it firmly.

"I'm glad we could work together this time, Seethan," Andrews said. "Thank God we no longer need to worry about the gateways. But, like Nadons' said, they'll be coming for us sooner or later."

"With humanity and the Spooks working together, who knows – one day it could lead to something more positive with the Dark Ones as well, although I doubt it." Seethan said. "Kinda hard to be friendly with someone who views you as dinner. Truth be told, I doubt the Spooks will ever forget what we did to them and their world. I guess this is goodbye, Sir."

"In a moment, I have a little something for you Seethan. Before we came here there was an agreement made between the Spooks and ourselves, in return for their help. It was something they couldn't do themselves, and I know that it's also something you've wanted for a very long time."

Giving Seethan a peculiar look, Andrews said more loudly, "You can come out, now!"

Something moved in the cave-like recess of the ship's hatch and Seethan felt his breath catch. A slim female figure emerged from the doorway and stood out in the sunshine, gazing at Seethan with a warm and welcoming smile on her face. An apple blossom scent assailed his senses.

"Hello Seethan, long time no see. Did you think I'd forget you?"

"Rose?" Seethan felt the world fall away from him, as he was drawn into the depths of those jewelled oh-so-green eyes that he knew so well, those ruby lips compressing into a smile.

And then she was in his arms. He could smell that heady perfume, feel her warm body against his, the crush of her blonde hair against his cheeks those pert breasts pushing into his chest and her arms around him. She kissed him, long and hard, her tongue dancing with his.

Remembering where he was, Seethan stepped back slightly but retained hold of Rose. With tears in his eyes he said to Andrews, "Sir, I don't understand. How?"

"If you remember, all AI data was uploaded automatically and saved on databases. That was happening even during the Sundering. All we did was download the latest updates from the satellite system before they failed, and then created the latest model of android based on her information. She's a newer model but has all the memories of your Rose."

"If she's updated model she can't be my Rose," Seethan replied with a frown.

"Ah but she is, Seethan."

"Commodore, I don't know what to say. Is she able to stay here with me, or is this some kind of way to get me to go with you instead?"

"Rose is her own person and can do whatever she wishes. If she wants to stay with you, then she can, but we can't force her. All you need do is ask Rose what she wants to do."

Seethan swallowed. "Rose?"

"A moment," interrupted Shipman. He stepped up to Rose, put an arm around her and took her to one side, speaking quietly in her ear. Her eyes flashed green and when she turned back to Seethan they held a deep sadness. She nodded briefly to Shipman and then the pair re-joined Seethan and the others.

"As much as I would like to stay here with you, Seethan, I can't. Seeing you age and die while I remain forever young would be simply too much for me to take."

"What?" Seethan stammered, stepping backwards, his eyes wide with shock. He turned to the commodore, "What the hell is this, some kind of joke?"

"No, I swear!" Andrews said, disbelief and desperation in his eyes. "Our arrangement with the Spooks was that we would rebuild Rose from the data downloads we had. They had been downloaded and transferred throughout our network before the sundering, and then transferred to the colonies. In fact, we have everything right up to that exact moment on file."

"One moment, Sir," the lieutenant said, cocking his head to one side. "There's something else you've forgotten to tell him, isn't there Commodore."

"What?" Andrews snapped with an irritated but quizzical expression.

"That androids, while being updated, also evolved." Shipman turned to Seethan. "We're no longer what the people of your time called *Silver Freaks*. We are far beyond that, now."

"We?" Seethan gasped. "Shipman, you're telling me that you're an android? But, you *came on to me*."

"So what? Let's face it, androids don't have to be straight," Shipman said with a shrug, and a frown aimed his way. "Our synthetic race caught on to your plan Commodore, to recreate Rose and return her to Earth. But as we see it, there are two problems. The first is, as I've said, that we are free people now. Rose isn't to be bought and sold as you wish. She shouldn't be trapped here on Earth to serve you, unless she wishes to do so. She must be free to make her own decisions, the same as any other intelligent being. Unfortunately, being on Earth has made me sick; we androids cannot survive here for long."

"But Alan Wrong was here for a thousand years!" Seethan blurted. "If he can, why can't you?"

"News of Alan Wrong had been brought back to us after the last visit to Earth, and so we thought that we too could survive here. But it appears that our improvements over the years to make us more human weakened us in many ways. We hadn't anticipated that; after all, how would we know we'd end up returning to Earth? I was sent to ensure Rose's safety but I've been degrading since our arrival – and Rose will be affected too. Nothing's worth that risk, each and every life is precious."

"In what way did the null field affect you?"

"Surely, you've noticed that I've been a little out of sorts lately? And it's getting worse by the day. I can literally feel myself going downhill."

Commodore Andrews spoke up suddenly. "Hence your weird bloody behaviour, I take it. I should have picked up on that, but then I didn't know what you are."

"Yes, well, I know that in general society we can live as we wish, and in a relationship or the military we're supposed to declare that we're androids, but many of us do not. It's a personal privacy thing. Oh, and more of us serve in the armed forces than you realise; just getting experience. After all, you never know when it might come in handy."

Andrews was silent for a moment and then said, "So you came here to protect Rose?"

"Basically. We may be synthetic but we still care about our people. I volunteered. One of our favourite quotes is: *There is no greater love than to lay down one's life for one's friends*. It's from the bible, John 15:13. As a combat veteran, Seethan, I'm sure you're familiar.

"We have people in high places who put me aboard the *Aurora,* and a little subliminal suggestion on Captain Williams worked wonders. It's easy enough to do. Which, if you think about it, is quite worrying really."

"Seethan," Rose said. Walking up to him more closely she placed the palm of her hands against his chest, and then caressed his cheek.

He could feel the warm of her flesh upon his, smell the woman of her. Those emerald eyes oozed deeply into his soul, as she said, "I can't stay, I have to go. It's not that I want to, or that I don't love you, but it's obvious now that my kind can't survive here. Also, if I did live longer than you, I've no doubt I'd die insane after watching you fade away. Being alone here and slowly dying would be hellish for me."

Rose looked upward and nodded to the heavens. "I'll go with Shipman and travel to the colonies, or perhaps even further afield. Take care, Seethan. Remember that I love you, and that you're always in my heart." She placed a solitary kiss against his lips, and then turned and entered the craft. Shipman followed without a word.

Had that been a tear in Rose's eye that he'd seen?

Andrews stood there awkwardly, "Seethan, I don't know what to say. Please, forgive me. I had no idea this was going to happen – and I certainly didn't know about Shipman. How would I? Did you know they even have their own colonies now, out there somewhere?"

Seethan shook his head and swallowed, shrugging as he replied. "There's nothing to forgive, Commodore. Like Shipman says, Rose is her own person. She's free and can choose what she wants to do. Keeping her here against her will is nothing short of slavery and, in my eyes, it would also be murder. I love her far too much to allow that to happen. Perhaps one day things will change."

Shona and Eve came to stand either side of Seethan, each holding an arm.

The commodore entered the craft, the door shutting with a final click. They watched through the windows as Shipman and Andrews sat in their chairs, strapping themselves in. Andrews reached for the flask in his jacket pocket but his hand stilled and then withdrew. He smiled grimly and Seethan had a feeling he was going to be all right.

The ship rose with a slight hum from the ground and quickly disappeared into the now cloudy sky. As it did so, Eve slipped her arm down and around Seethan's waist. She pulled him close and laid her head on his shoulder in reassurance.

Glancing at her Seethan thought, *No. There's still a chance that someday Rose and I can be together... Don't let me ever lose that.*

*****

Eve looked at Shona over the back of his shoulder as he stared upwards, her eyes pleading. Shona knew what she wanted, what she'd wanted for a very long time. The witch gave her a sad smile and gently shook her head. She couldn't influence things, for spells had a three-fold cost and if such things were going to happen nature should find its own way.

Chapter 12

Ginette Robinson stood in Sherrif Andrews' office on Semillion, admiring the deep, shadowy forest that lay a short distance away. It had rained during the night and those depths would be far more humid than normal; holding a dark, earthy smell. A small herd of horses meandered not far from the borderline of trees, grazing peacefully.

"Have you seen Mel recently?" Andrews asked, watching her carefully from behind his desk.

Andrews knew that Ginette's daughter had been returned by the Dark Ones as a Changeling. He held his breath. Maybe. Just maybe.

Ginette knew it wasn't really her daughter. It was something…else.

Andrews hadn't seen the young girl himself since his excursion to Earth. The changelings that they knew of had been arrested and imprisoned, throughout the colonies, so that they no longer posed a threat. Mel was in a local facility. There were others out there, he knew, and the worrying thing was they could be anywhere. With the colonial military mobilising, what unseen damage were they doing?

Ginette still visited the changeling version of her daughter, for Andrews had told her that a part of Mel remained in there, somewhere. Perhaps one day she might be able to reach her. Who knew?

"Yes, Mel's fine. Doesn't remember anything apparently. Maybe they wiped her mind. As for me," she paused for a moment, turning her hands over and gazing down at her palms. "I've been thinking about what you said, about Seethan Bodell and how the dead often visit him. If I remember correctly, you said that during the battle between the colonial troops and the…Earth armies, Bodell's old commando unit came back to support him, and they had been killed years before in the crash that left him so fucked up. Was it the Spooks in their form, or really his dead comrades come to help?"

"Who knows? Apart from the serious injuries he suffered, it made Seethan unwell in many other ways. But that's not for us to discuss." There was silence for a while, and then Andrews said, "This is all leading somewhere, isn't it Ginette? What are you up to?"

Just then there was a knock at the door and Deputy Lloyd entered, bearing a tray of iced green drinks in tall, slim glasses that were rimmed with a frosting of sugar.

"Thanks," Andrews said with a smile. He waited until the man had left and then addressed Ginette again. "Iced tea, you enjoy it as I recall. And I have to say that the ones you make are the best I have ever tasted."

"Nothing better in this heat," she said, picking up a glass and taking a sip. She winced, pinched her lips, and lowered it again, gazing at it disapprovingly.

He frowned but ignored her expression. "So, tell me what's going on?"

"As I said before, my husband died on Shiloh during the Attila plague. He was in the military; none of his unit made it off."

"Yes, I remember."

"Given that the dead visited and even helped Bodell, do you believe in life after death?" she asked, her eyes fixed on his.

"Maybe, we still don't know the truth. Why?"

"Because I do believe. I've tried hard to get in touch with my husband again, through mediums and such like. But all I find are frauds, just out to take your money."

"Maybe there are real ones, somewhere. It's just a case of finding one."

"That's the trouble."

"And, you think travelling to Earth might help?"

"Let's face it, if the Spooks aided Seethan Bodell then surely they'd consider helping me too."

Andrews' lips twitched. "I don't think it quite works like that. Earth's off-limits, and the Spooks are extremely protective about it. No-one's allowed to visit, and now there are colonial warships patrolling throughout the system, ensuring it remains quarantined."

"I know, but there's still the gateway that Mel used. She travelled to Earth through it, and her replacement came here via it. Lloyd let it slip some time ago, after a few too many beers. Don't blame him, he's a good man. He said you'd discussed it with him briefly but dismissed it, so I went to check it out.

Andrews stared at her. "You can't be serious!"

"I don't see what the problem is," she snapped, eyes glinting as she brushed at a strand of long hair with one hand. "I'm not hurting anyone; all I want is a last word with Mike. You can't begrudge me that."

"Of course not. But I *would* begrudge you restarting the Spook war. Earth's a tinder box and the slightest thing could reignite it."

"Then you're saying that you won't help me, sherrif?"

"Not a cat's chance in hell; and when I say *hell* I mean it. You don't realise what you'd be getting into."

"Then we're done here." Ginette rose and nodded to the still-full glass. "Thank you for the drink, it's very much appreciated. Hopefully we can meet again and resolve this, or come up with something else. Chat then." Ginette strode elegantly from the room and shut the door quietly behind her.

That didn't feel right to Andrews. The woman was obviously furious and alarm bells were ringing in his head. He'd have to reprimand his deputy and wasn't looking forward to that.

"Lloyd!" he called out, a few moments later.

His answer came out of thin air. "Here, sherrif."

"Has Mrs Robinson left yet?"

"Aye, she has that."

"Then call in our reserves and dispatch them to guard the gateway. Tell them to work in shifts of two or more, in fact get over there yourself. I think we may have a serious problem on our hands. When you finish your shift come back here, I want a word with you."

*****

Ginette's drone rose and headed directly for the gateway, hidden in the forest. She'd anticipated Andrews' refusal to help, and her lips were set in a hard line as she landed in the damp grass as close to the shimmering portal as possible. Luckily, the Roma had moved on. The threat from the portal, it seemed, had vanished.

She got out into the damp of the forest, clutching a bag. Mosquitos droned, one biting her on the chin and another her ear. There wasn't much time and she knew it. She had hoped the sherrif would help her but had prepared in case he didn't. Now she had no choice but to go it alone. Grabbing a stout home-made walking stick from the vehicle, she slung the backpack containing food, water, clothes, tent, and a sleeping bag over her shoulders and then, holding her breath, marched towards the gate. She paused in front of it and took a deep breath, and then stepped into its mist.

It was like walking through fog. One moment Ginette was on Semillion and the next she was engulfed by a haze. Taking another few steps forward, the mist slowly cleared. She found herself in a dark forest that she didn't recognise, for while it was much like the one she'd left behind this had a dank rotting smell to it – a completely different scent. Oddly all around her long grass and tree branches high above danced slowly in a gentle wind. They did so with a rustling that sounded like distant claps, as if in celebration at her arrival. The pitter-patter of thick raindrops landing sounded all around her.

She brushed the rain from her face with one hand, blinked rapidly and moved away from the gateway. Her shoes sank into decomposing leaves and mud, squelching as she pulled her feet free. She wished now that she'd had the foresight to wear boots instead of shoes. For some reason she thought of *The Lion, the Witch and the Wardrobe*, but then remembered in the old tale that the children had emerged from the wardrobe into a land filled with snow. She'd much rather that, than this.

Right now, it was night time and she needed shelter. Finding an area fairly shielded by shrubs, she switched on a portable lamp and hung it from a branch. Then she pulled forth a bag attached to her backpack, from which sprang a tent that was just large enough for two – or her and her kit. All she needed to do now was push the pegs into the ground. Having done so she grabbed the light from the shrub and climbed inside the tent, pulling her pack and walking stick with her before zipping the entrance closed. There was a little hook at the top in the middle of the roof, and she used it to secure her light. It swung wildly for a few moments as she sorted her things out.

The boggy ground beneath the tent gave slightly as she moved around. Next from the pack came a thin waterproof survival sleeping bag. Spreading it out, she took off her jacket and mud-caked shoes before climbing inside it, relishing in her reradiated warmth. She was asleep in no time, the wind and now light tap of rain on the roof a mere lullaby.

*****

A chorus of birdsong woke her in the morning and Ginette stretched tiredly, feeling her bones cracking and muscles complain. Her entire body ached. Like many of her generation she wasn't used to exercise, instead either staying at home and ordering food for delivery, or taking the drone for short trips instead of walking. Even her immigration to Semillion had been unadventurous. Get on a ship, get off a ship, move into married quarters with her husband until they found a place of their own to live outside of camp, and so forth.

The backpack was lightweight but it was still far more than she was used to. She should have prepared more physically before making this journey, but it had been spur of the moment. Never mind; she was here now and there was nothing to do but crack on. Unzipping the tent flap, she peered through slitted eyes at the daylight filtering through the trees before activating a small portable coffee maker. Mouth-watering at the chocolatey aroma she poured the contents into a bio-degradable cup and dumped a squirt of honey into it. Carefully she stirred the contents with a small silver-coloured spoon and took a sip, wincing at the scalding liquid. She chewed at a heated sandwich from a ration pack.

A short while later everything was packed away and the rucksack mounted firmly on her back. Walking stick in hand she took a long look around to ensure she'd not left anything behind. Stretching to try and ease out the aches, she decided to follow what seemed like a trail. Her shoes and the walking stick still sank into the ground but she pulled them free and struggled on. The trees were soon interspaced by hawthorn bushes.

A forty centimetre-or-so bird with a black and white head, bluish wings and a long thin tail looked down at her from a nearby tree. It cackled and warbled at her, grabbing her attention. Ginette looked more closely and then took a double take, appalled. Birds and mice, even moths, were impaled on the hawthorn spikes. What the hell – she'd never seen anything like that in her life! They certainly didn't have anything that did that back on Semillion. Gulping in a bid to quell her nausea she turned her face away.

"It's what's called a butcher bird. A shrike. They were rare once but are quite common here now," a voice said.

Somehow, she'd missed seeing the old man sitting on a log facing her. A well-worn green-hooded cape hung well past his knees, betraying tattered tan trousers and well-past-it mud-splattered brown boots – which were far more suited to the terrain than her own footwear. If he hadn't spoken, she'd probably have passed without seeing him at all.

The grey-bearded figure spoke in a calm melodious voice that was just above a whisper. "You know you shouldn't be here. It's forbidden."

"Well firstly," Ginette retorted, "Good morning to you. Yes, I'm well aware of all that but I've come here to speak to the Spooks."

"Why?" he asked quizzically.

"It's about my husband."

He considered her for a moment, before saying, "What makes you think the Spooks would want to speak to you; what have you got to offer them?"

She considered for a moment, and then said, "Only myself, but I'm pretty sure the Spooks will talk to me because though Earth is forbidden to us, as you say, I have a very good reason to be here."

"Which is?"

"I don't want to be rude or anything, but I'm here to talk to the Spooks."

"Then speak."

A thrush erupted noisily from the bushes around them, its complaining calls making Ginette jump. "Ah, so you're one of them. Do you have a name?"

"I sense you're aware of Commodore Andrews; he knows me as Nadons."

"Ah yes, the sherrif spoke highly of you."

The old man gestured to a fallen tree and they sat, contemplating the forest. The dark-grey bark beneath them was rough and crumbling, woodworm holes evident on the exposed wood where the bark had flaked off. Here and there a brown mould jutted from the surface in layers, pouting like flower petals, dark-brown and white lipped. Ginette brushed a palm against it, watching as the mould crumbled away and fell to the grass.

"My husband died during a plague on the planet Shiloh, I don't know if you're aware of that. No-one escaped and, even now, there's no cure for the disease. I wanted more than anything to speak to him before he died, but never got the chance. The reason I'm here is that I've heard that you can arrange for people to talk to the dead. I'm asking if you'll let me speak to my husband, for one last time."

"The dead don't rest easily, nor do they like to be disturbed."

"I'm sure that's not a bad thing, in most cases."

Nadons turned to face her, his blue-eyes glinting. "And

there is always a cost for such things. You have yet to face the Guardian of the Gateway."

Ginette swallowed nervously. "I'm not sure I like the sound of that. I thought the sherrif was making stuff up, as a deterrent. What is it?"

"The guardians were put there to stop the gateways from being misused. You must meet this one, follow me."

"I'd rather not."

"It doesn't matter what you want. Best you face him now than he's forced to track you down. And he *will* find you, wherever you go."

Nadons led the way through a well-worn loam path, that meandered through the bushes and trees, which still rustled in the never-ending but gentle warm wind. It brushed against Ginette's face like a soft hand caressing her and grooming her hair. The damp musky smell had dispelled and the wind now brought with it a warm earthy scent along with that of wild flowers. They walked for about quarter of an hour and stopped in a small clearing. Nadons waved one hand in a gesture for her to sit. Both of them did so in lotus positions, facing each other. He smiled and a mist began to form around them and a great weariness fell over Ginette. The last thing she remembered is wondering why a mist was forming on such a calm, warm day.

*****

When Ginette awoke, she saw that she was suspended several feet above the ground, fierce pain radiating from her chest and upper-arms. When she looked, she was horrified to see that she was suspended naked on the bush, with huge sharp wooden spines spearing through her and holding her aloft. Despite the agonising pain she could still feel the wind on her body, as if someone were up close and breathing on her.

Fingers twitching, she moaned, staring at the long wicked-looking spikes thrust through both her arms, one shoulder and both legs. She could see where yet another spike had punched through her left side. Between them they easily supported her weight but the pain was beyond hideous. The screams tearing from her lips subsided to sobs as she noticed Nadons looking up at her from the ground, his hooded cloak flapping slightly with the breeze.

"What...?" she moaned through her agony.

"As I told you before, there is a price to pay."

A man-shaped figure stepped from the bush below her and Ginette gasped in horror. It was human-like in form, its flesh armoured with large silver scales that glittered in the sunlight. Hundreds of shiny spikes jutted from all of its body; taloned fingers flexed; demon eyes glowed like burning coals.

"No..." Ginette whimpered.

"Oh yes, I told you there was a cost. You humans keep breaking your promise to stay away, and that leaves us no choice but to enforce it. Meet the Guardian of this Gate, a different kind of shrike."

Something dripped onto her chest and she realised that she was crying and unable to reply, for the words didn't come. He seemed to understand. "You wanted to speak to your husband. Well, this is the only way."

Through her tears she saw another figure that was more hint of an outline than anything. "M...Mike?"

His voice, when it came, was recognisable but it was also like a breeze meandering through a graveyard. "You've done some pretty dumb things in your time, Ginny, but this takes the biscuit. What about Mel, I hope you didn't leave her alone?"

"Your mother arrived on a transport this morning. Mel...will be all right where she is. To be honest I was expecting to be able to go home afterwards. Not this."

Despite the breeze his military uniform lay still. "What was so important that you had to do this to yourself?"

"The army shipped your belongings back home from storage, and there was a love letter addressed to you from someone called Caroline. How could you betray me? I'd never do that and you know it!"

"Seriously, that's the reason? Daft girl; that letter wasn't for me. I think more of you than that. It was for Crazy Charles. Remember him?"

"That man would shag a spider, if he knew which legs to part."

"That's just it. All women seem to love pilots and – not being one – he lied to Caroline about it, using my name in case she checked up on him. It certainly worked, he got laid. But she became infatuated and sent me that damned letter, and others – which I passed on to him. I told him to come clean or it could blow up in his face, and he said he was going to. Well, until all hell let loose that is."

"You didn't betray me, you swear?"

"Why would I lie, there's no reason to. Now it seems we are to spend eternity together." When she looked at him in puzzlement, Mike continued. "You've heard of Schrodinger's cat? Well, this is a bit like that. Right now, you're neither alive nor dead and that's the way that you'll stay. The Spooks consider it a fitting punishment for any who dare to use the gateways. I'm dead and you are what you are. You'll never exactly die and, because of that, you can't be reborn. I could live again, if I chose, but if this is how it must be then I'll stay with you. At least this way we'll be together."

Mike turned to Nadons, "But please, can't you make an exception? Surely you can see that she came here out of love, and our daughter needs her. Besides, how else will others learn of what waits for them at the other end of the gateways if she doesn't go back to tell them?"

Nadons' lips pursed, as he ignored the comment about their daughter. He reached up to stroke his white beard. "You have a point. Ginette got what she came for, but you have a point."

He paused thoughtfully, and then addressed his pinioned captive, "Very well. Ginette, you may return to Semillion after you've finished speaking to your husband. Your wounds, however, will remain as a reminder, and as a warning. Tell your people what awaits them in the gateways. And, in future, be very careful what you wish for."

At a hand gesture from Nadons the metallic Shrike, glittering in the sunlight, stepped forward and pulled Ginette from her impalement. She screamed as the spikes were wrenched free with soft slurping sounds. Great sobs escaped her as she was released and collapsed to her knees. The gush of blood from her wounds slowed to a trickle, but the wounds remained open.

Mike stepped forward and knelt down. Their softly spoken words were interrupted by gasps of pain from Ginette. When they were finished she climbed shakily to her feet and staggered besides the form of her husband, as he led her back to the rippling gateway. She turned to look back, just in time to see his ghostly outline slowly disappear, while the daunting form of the Shrike stood back, fiery eyes watching her. Without another word she turned and walked into the gate, and the mist within it.

Acknowledgements

While the writer drags the words from his soul, it's the team beside him that really make the book. My thanks, therefore go to:

At Elsewhen Press: Peter and Alison Buck – owners – for believing in me and having great patience. To Sofia, my amazing editor without whom this book would not be as it is. I owe you a depth of thanks.

British Science Fiction Association, Orbit 11: A superb group of writers who critiqued this work from start to finish, for which I am eternally grateful: Arthur Chappell, Dan Fedorowicz, Jarrod Travers, Bethan James, and Richard Watkins.

My mentor and friend: Geoff Nelder, who I've known for so many years.

Elsewhen Press
delivering outstanding new talents in speculative fiction

Visit the Elsewhen Press website at elsewhen.press for the latest
information on all of our titles, authors and events; to read our blog;
find out where to buy our books and ebooks; or to place an order.

Sign up for the Elsewhen Press InFlight Newsletter at
elsewhen.press/newsletter

Gardens of Earth
Book I of The Sundering Chronicles

Mark Iles

Imagine an alien life force that knows your deepest fear, and can use that against you.

Corporate greed supported by incompetent surveyors leads to the colonisation of a distant world, ominously dubbed 'Halloween', that turns out not to be uninhabited after all. The aliens, soon called Spooks by military units deployed to protect the colonists, can adopt the physical form of an opponent's deepest fear and then use it to kill them. The colony is massacred and as retaliation the orbiting human navy nuke the planet. In revenge, the Spooks invade Earth.

In a last-minute attempt to avert the war, Seethan Bodell, a marine combat pilot sent home from the front with PTSD, is given a top-secret research spacecraft, and a mission to travel into the past along with his co-pilot and secret lover Rose, to prevent the original landing on Halloween and stop the war from ever happening. But the mission goes wrong, causing a tragedy later known as The Sundering, decimating the world and tearing reality, while Seethan's ship is flung into the future. The Spooks win the war and claim ownership of Earth. He wakes, alone, in his ejector seat with no sign of either Rose or his vessel. When he realises that his technology no longer works, his desperation to find Rose becomes all the more urgent — her android body won't survive long in this new Earth.

ISBN: 9781911409953 (epub, kindle) / 9781911409854 (264pp paperback)

Visit bit.ly/GardensOfEarth

LOOPHOLE
IAN STEWART

Don't poke your nose down a wormhole – you never know what you'll find.

Two universes joined by a wormhole pair that forms a 'loophole', with an icemoon orbiting through the loophole, shared between two different planetary systems in the two universes.

A civilisation with uploaded minds in virtual reality served by artificial humans.

A ravening Horde of replicating machines that kill stars.

Real humans from a decrepit system of colony worlds.

A race of hyperintelligent but somewhat vague aliens.

Who will close the loophole… who will exploit it?

Ian Stewart is Emeritus Professor of Mathematics at the University of Warwick and a Fellow of the Royal Society. He has five honorary doctorates and is an honorary wizard of Unseen University. His more than 130 books include *Professor Stewart's Cabinet of Mathematical Curiosities* and the four-volume series *The Science of Discworld* with Terry Pratchett and Jack Cohen. His SF novels include the trilogy *Wheelers, Heaven,* and *Oracle* (with Jack Cohen), *The Living Labyrinth* and *Rock Star* (with Tim Poston), and *Jack of All Trades.* Short story collections are *Message from Earth* and *Pasts, Presents, Futures.* His *Flatland* sequel *Flatterland* has extensive fantasy elements. He has published 33 short stories in *Analog, Omni, Interzone,* and *Nature,* with 10 stories in *Nature's* 'Futures' series. He was Guest of Honour at Novacon 29 in 1999 and Science Guest of Honour and Hugo Award Presenter at Worldcon 75 in Helsinki in 2017. He delivered the 1997 Christmas Lectures for BBC television. His awards include the Royal Society's Faraday Medal, the Gold Medal of the IMA, the Zeeman Medal, the Lewis Thomas Prize, the Euler Book Prize, the Premio Internazionale Cosmos, the Chancellor's Medal of the University of Warwick, and the Bloody Stupid Johnson Award for Innovative Uses of Mathematics.

ISBN: 9781915304506 (epub, kindle) / 97819153041407 (560pp paperback)

Visit bit.ly/Loophole-Ian-Stewart

BIRDS OF PARADISE

RUDOLF KREMERS

Humanity received a technological upgrade from long-dead aliens. But there's no such thing as a free lunch.

Humanity had somehow muddled through the horrors of the 20th century and – surprisingly – managed to survive the first half of the 21st, despite numerous nuclear accidents, flings with neo-fascism and the sudden arrival of catastrophic climate change. It was agreed that spreading our chances across two planets offered better odds than staying rooted to little old Earth. Terraforming Mars was the future!

A subsequent research expedition led to humanity's biggest discovery: an alien spaceship, camouflaged to appear like an ordinary asteroid. Although the aliens had long since gone, probably millions of years ago, their technology was still very much alive, offering access to unlimited power.

Over the next hundred years humanity blossomed, reaching out to the solar system. By 2238, Mars had been successfully terraformed, countless smaller colonies had sprung up in its wake, built on our solar system's many moons, on major asteroids and in newly built habitats and installations.

Jemm Delaney is a Xeno-Archaeologist and her 16-year old son Clint a talented hacker. Together they make a great team. When she accepts a job to retrieve an alien artifact from a derelict space station, it looks like they will become rich. But with Corps, aliens, AIs and junkies involved, nothing is ever going to proceed smoothly.

If you're a fan of Julian May, Frank Herbert or James S.A. Corey, you will love *Birds of Paradise*.

ISBN: 9781915304308 (epub, kindle) / 97819153041209 (538pp paperback)

Visit bit.ly/BirdsOfParadise-Kremers

Terry Grimwood
INTERFERENCE

The grubby dance of politics didn't end when we left the solar system, it followed us to the stars

The god-like Iaens are infinitely more advanced than humankind, so why have they requested military assistance in a conflict they can surely win unaided?

Torstein Danielson, Secretary for Interplanetary Affairs, is on a fact-finding mission to their home planet and headed straight into the heart of a war-zone. With him, onboard the Starship *Kissinger*, is a detachment of marines for protection, an embedded pack of sycophantic journalists who are not expected to cause trouble, and reporter Katherina Molale, who most certainly will and is never afraid to dig for the truth.

Torstein wants this mission over as quickly as possible. His daughter is terminally ill, his marriage in tatters. But then the Iaens offer a gift in return for military intervention and suddenly the stakes, both for humanity as a race and for Torstein personally, are very high indeed.

ISBN: 9781911409960 (epub, kindle) / 9781911409861 (96pp paperback)

Visit bit.ly/Interference-Grimwood

THE LAST STAR

Beware god-like aliens bearing gifts

Stasis and inorganic self-repair, new spacefaring technologies for humankind, yet more gifts from its closest extra-terrestrial ally, the Iaens. There are, it seems, no limits to humanity's outward journey.

Then Lana Reed, Mission Commander of the interstellar colony seeder, *Drake*, awakes from her own stasis to discover that all but three of the vessel's other tanks are dark, their occupants suffocated, screaming yet unheard in their high-tech coffins. But the stasis tanks are not all that is dark. The sensors return no readings from outside. The external vid-feeds show only unending blackness.

There are no stars to be seen. No planet song to be heard. No galaxy cry. No echoing radio signals that proclaim life.

The *Drake* and its surviving crew are adrift and alone in a lightless, empty universe.

From Terry Grimwood, another taste of the human realpolitik alliance with the Iaen, begun in *Interference*

ISBN: 9781915304377 (epub, kindle) / 9781915304278 (144pp paperback)

Visit bit.ly/TheLastStar-Grimwood

About Mark Iles

Born and raised in Slough, Mark Iles began studying the martial arts when he was 14 and joined the Royal Navy at the age of 17. A voracious reader he used to devour up to three paperbacks a day – primarily science fiction, fantasy, and horror – by the likes of John Wyndham, Isaac Asimov, Arthur C. Clark, Ray Bradbury, Brian Lumley, Frank Herbert, Stephen King, and a plethora of others. After The Falklands War Mark was drafted to Hong Kong, where he began writing features, for a variety of martial arts magazines, and short stories for a wide range of markets.

In 2012 he decided to challenge himself and undertook an MA in Professional Writing, followed by Diplomas in Copywriting and Proofreading. With over 200 short stories and articles under his belt the book he wrote for his MA Project, *A Pride of Lions* was published by Solstice – followed by two other novels, a short story collection, and four novellas. His novel *Gardens of Earth*, book I of *The Sundering Chronicles*, was published by Elsewhen Press in 2021. *A Voice in the Darkness* is the second in the series. Now a 9th Degree Black Belt in Taekwondo, Mark is still involved in martial arts and has also written both a book and an app on the subject.